D1557407

THE GHOST OF Bud Parrott

Bud Parrott, c. 1950

THE GHOST OF Bud Parrott

A NOVEL

JUDSON N. HOUT

Parkhurst Brothers, Inc., Publishers
LITTLE ROCK

PARKHURST BROTHERS, INC., PUBLISHERS

www.pbros.net

Parkhurst Brothers books are distributed to the trade through the Chicago Distribution Center, a unit of the University of Chicago Press, and may be ordered through Ingram Book Company, Baker & Taylor, Follett Library Resources and other book industry wholesalers. To order from the University of Chicago's Chicago Distribution Center, phone 1-800-621-2736 or send a fax to 1-800-621-8476. Copies of this and other Parkhurst Brothers, Inc., Publishers titles are available to organizations and corporations for purchase in quantity by contacting Special Sales Department at our home office location, listed on our website.

This is a work of the author's imagination, a work of fiction.

Printed in Canada

First Edition, 2011

2011 2012 2013 2014 2015 2016   16 15 14 13 12 11 10 9 8 7 6 5 4 3 2 1

Library of Congress Control Number: Consult www.pbros.net/hout

ISBN: Hardback Edition: 978-1-935166-37-5   [10 digit: 1-935166-37-9]

Design Director and Dustjacket/cover design:
Wendell E. Hall

Page design:
Shelly Culbertson

Acquired for Parkhurst Brothers and edited by:
Ted Parkhurst

Proofreaders:
Barbara and Bill Paddack

Dedicated to my wife,

Carolyn,

without whose encouragement

I would not have attempted to write

acknowledgements

I owe a deep debt of gratitude to many friends and family members who read the early drafts of this novel and encouraged me to push forward toward completion and publication. Each of you is dear to me; your kind words have kept me to the task when my own spirit was tired. Sandra Tribble transformed my sheets of handwritten text into the requisite computer files and cleanly printed pages until we had it right. Her patience and faithfulness are beyond measure. John Minor found the photograph of the real Bud Parrott, who inspired this work of fiction. Frank Plegge reproduced the photograph in a form suitable for publication. I would also like to thank Mary Catherine of mc photography for the photograph on the back jacket of this book.

My late mother-in-law, Margaret Lindsey, read the manuscript and encouraged me to complete it, a gift of faith for which I'll be eternally grateful. Likewise, my late brother, Phil Hout, supported me when I needed it most. We in Camden, Arkansas, are fortunate to have Lynne Rowland and her Book & Frame Shop; I am especially indebted for her recommendation of this work to its publisher.

Ted Parkhurst, publisher at Parkhurst Brothers, Inc., risks his reputation and his resources by publishing my work, a leap of faith and investment of capital that I do not take for granted. Roger Armbrust (who agreed to allow my work to impose upon an already full publishing schedule), Barbara and Bill Paddack (for their careful proofreading), Buster Hall (for his inspired cover design) and Shelly Culbertson (for her elegant page design) have each contributed their support and talent to this work. We are fortunate to have their talents publishing new books in our time.

foreword

This novel, this work of fiction, is the result of my affection for the time and place in which I grew up: Northeast Arkansas in the 1940s mostly. I have chosen to use the real name of a man who was my friend and confidant in those days, Bud Parrott. I knew Bud Parrott late in his life. He taught me a great deal about being a man in this world. Although he lived with my family for eight years, I learned nothing of his past. There were rumors that he had played Negro League baseball in his youth, rumors he would neither confirm nor deny. He could, however, throw a sharply breaking curve ball, a skill he tried to teach me without success. When I decided to write a novel, I chose to make Bud the hero and picture him as I imagined his life might have been. In doing this, I have completed a work that is purely and totally fiction.

In all the years Bud was close to me, I felt I never really knew him. His outward jovial, cheerful personality seemed to mask a deeper sadness. As far as any of us knew, he had no relatives.

In writing of that time and place, I have felt it was important to use the deplorable N-word in places. It is not used to offend the reader, but rather to be true to the period and place. I hope the reader will understand and accept that for what it is.

Judson N. Hout
Camden, Arkansas, 2010

I am haunted by a menagerie of memories of childhood. Pleasant and unpleasant, the days of my youth have been tumbled in a drum of years. Days of excitement, anticipation and discovery are jumbled up with events so frightening I wish they would go away. Some days from those years so long ago often do seem buried in some New Orleans-style vault, away somewhere, yet not quite out of consciousness. Always, they are floating in my subconscious ready to pierce the veil of knowing.

From the day I walked out of Newport, the county seat that had been my home in Northeast Arkansas, in 1953, I have poked and prodded those ghosts whenever they threatened entry into my daily thoughts. Now the time had come to brave the place again, to travel back into the Delta, to see Newport one last time. To resurrect the ghost of Bud Parrott required a bold attempt to burying the others, once and for all.

A girl from Kirkwood, a suburb of St. Louis, Missouri, appeared in Newport the summer of my fifteenth year. Brenda Langston was unlike any girl in Newport: sophisticated beyond her years, composed with a style that drew me like a moth to the lantern. I was profoundly

9

grateful that it was my good fortune to live in the town in which she visited her grandmother. One year I visited her in Kirkwood, her elegant world that seemed to me like an Emerald City. From that experience on, I knew St. Louis was where I wanted to live when I was grown and on my own.

The world of business was unkind to many during my working years, chewing up their days and spitting out their dreams. In spite of the childhood memories that threatened to cloud my own working days, somehow rewards seemed to find me. Oh, I worked hard, but planning never really was my thing. A happy accident, that's how I thought of my career: a scene written by a cosmic committee in which I was drafted to play. In the end, I owned my own brokerage firm in St. Louis. I lived in the very best neighborhood. My car was envied by neighbors; my wardrobe announced a man of substance. A corps of subordinates kept my calendar, served my meals, and arranged my philanthropies.

The grave of the old black man I last saw forty-nine years ago, in the summer of 1953 — that's what pulled me back to Newport. Old myself now, I felt the need to be close to him one more time before I died. I left my staff behind and drove myself south along the Mississippi. Being alone in a car was new to me, and I liked the freedom of it, in spite of the needles that swam beneath my collarbone. Like the needles on each side of a catfish chin, I thought, swimming there between my clavicle and my heart.

I saw his ghost two months earlier.

I had gone in for my annual physical, and for the first time my cardiogram was abnormal. The old ticker, my doctor said, needed more study. A seriously abnormal stress test followed, and finally a coronary arteriogram showed what my doctor called a high-grade critical blockage. A heart attack at that spot would invariably be fatal, so I had no choice but to submit to bypass surgery.

My last memory, prior to surgery, was being moved onto a gurney in my room and being pushed by a pretty nurse down the hall, toward an operating room. The next thing I knew an intensely bright white light was all I could see, and I was unable to move. Scared — I was alarmed. Then, for no apparent reason, a strange quiet settled in my heart; I was at peace.

The light was vaguely comforting. I decided this was "the light," and I was dying and on my way to somewhere beautiful. Then I saw an indistinct figure shrouded in white. At first, I could not identify the figure. Gradually, a soft brown color developed at the head, and soon I recognized the face as that of Bud Parrott.

The apparition said nothing, but looked at me softly and tenderly. Gradually an awareness not of words, but of meanings, came over me. "Fire" and "steel" and "ain't your time yet, boy" were there in the room with me, not heard, not exactly thought, but there.

Then the apparition slowly dissolved, and the intense white light became two large overhead spotlights and four sets of long fluorescent ceiling lights. I heard a nurse say, "Your operation is over, Mr. Wood. You're doing fine. Just relax, everything is okay."

My hospital recuperation was uneventful, and Rachel, my wife, made my convalescence at home warm, with her homemade chicken noodle soup, and mellow, playing Miles Davis on the stereo. However, the apparition of Bud Parrot danced in the rotating blades of my ceiling fan. He sang to me, extended a hand I once reached out to grasp, and adjusted his cap, under which his knowing eyes sparkled.

By the time my strength returned, the idea of a trip back to the Newport of my youth seemed a fact of life, not an idea of mine.

Finding Bud's grave was just the thing to do. I hoped that his ghost could help me bury all the other haunts in my head. His extended hand was needed one last time.

By the time I reached Festus I decided if I were to make this trip into my past I should go the old way, the way I took when I was coming to St. Louis to court Brenda so many years ago. I left the interstate and took Highway 67, but it was at Fredericktown before it became the old two lane that I remembered.

From there on it was as though it were 1951 again — on down through Poplar Bluff and into Arkansas at Corning, then to Pocahontas and Walnut Ridge and Tuckerman and finally to Newport.

All along the way, I saw old abandoned tourist courts and filling stations decaying between the Walmarts, McDonalds and 7-Eleven stores. Occasionally the skeleton of a drive-in movie screen could be seen as a mournful reminder of those old passion pits of the fifties.

Those mid-century relics affected my mood, and at times, I could actually feel the ambiance of the past. The familiarity of the old road, though not traveled by me in over forty years, contributed to that feeling.

By the time I arrived in Newport I was in a somber and reflective mood, but I found the little town drastically changed from what I remembered.

There was no longer the old charm to the place. All the businesses, hospitals and nice homes were now east and north of the lake that bisects the town. The downtown business area of my youth was a shambles of wrecked, burned or caved-in buildings. The

Missouri-Pacific train station was abandoned. All that remained were some churches, law offices, the courthouse and a few second-rate businesses.

Homes of people I once knew and loved were now slum dwellings, and my childhood home at 19 Third Street had obviously stood empty for years.

All this left me sad, but I was determined to fulfill my quest and find the gravesite of my old friend and mentor.

Before searching for the grave, I had to explore my boyhood home. The house was a sorry sight. It had once been rather charming, if not stately. The style was a cross between English Tudor and what would later be called ranch-style. The facade was dark brick, and the shape was rectangular. The house had been built in 1927, and the lot covered almost a fourth of a block. When we moved into the house in 1941, there was still a concrete cistern out back as well as two concrete watering troughs for the former owner's horses.

A massive oak door opened to the foyer, and an ornate staircase on the right side of the room led to a second story that was unfinished and used as an attic. To the left was a large living room, with a fireplace. From that room, French doors led to a small sunroom where our Christmas trees were to be placed in years to come. To the right of the foyer was the dining room, and past it was a small breakfast room. Passing through the foyer to the left of the staircase one entered a long back hall at the left end of which was the large master bedroom, dressing room and bath. At the right end of the hall was a small bedroom, off which was a small bath. Through the small bedroom was a tiny laundry. Next was the kitchen, which also opened to the breakfast room. The back door from the kitchen led to a small, screened porch. To the left was a tiny utility room with a coal-burning furnace.

The back yard was very large and contained several large pecan trees. To the north was a small alley, and in the back yard adjacent to the alley was a long narrow rectangular frame building. The first two rooms of the building were servants' quarters and were suitable for a man and wife. Next came a room used as a smokehouse, then a tiny bathroom and finally a small room suitable for a single servant. None of these rooms were in use when my family moved in, and my father subsequently had the front two rooms made over into a garage for his car.

I could not believe the state of disrepair I found the house and grounds to be in. The garage and servant room were gone. Bricks were falling off the chimney of the abandoned house. The once manicured lawn was now overgrown with weeds and nettle grass.

The front door of the house was ajar, and when I entered, I was appalled. Cheap worn-out carpet covered the once lovely hardwood floors. The mantle was gone. Inexpensive remodeling had altered the floor plan drastically. Laminated paneling covered the plaster walls and had been installed by some very inept carpenter. The upstairs had been finished and made into a large bedroom with no windows. The quality of workmanship and materials was no better upstairs than downstairs.

A foul odor permeated the house, and everywhere were cobwebs and dirt. In one corner of the living room was a large pile of petrified dog feces.

As depressing as the place was, I found myself not wanting to leave. My ghosts were nearer now and my mood was most somber. Memories that should be happy were only sad — if not outright mournful. Here my ghosts had been born; here they would have to be buried.

14

By the time I left the house it was getting dark, so I checked into a motel for the night. While dining in the adjoining restaurant I saw several faces that were vaguely familiar but no one I was certain I knew.

I did strike up a conversation with an aging waitress, who told me that the unnamed cemetery where all the black people were buried was just down the road from Walnut Grove Cemetery where my parents and the rest of the white people were buried. After a rather fitful and dream-filled night, morning arrived. I showered and shaved and headed for the cemetery, taking with me my morning coffee in a Styrofoam cup. Upon arriving at Walnut Grove, I entered through the main gate to visit my parents' graves. The cemetery was very well kept with manicured lawns and tasteful gravestones. Flowers and shrubs were everywhere, and many and varied trees provided ample shade.

A wide plain headstone engraved simply "Wood" marked my parents' graves. Foot markers identified the couple as:

Isaac Henry Wood
Born May 14, 1911
Died Dec. 5, 1966

and

Naomi McDaniel Wood
Born June 1, 1914
Died Sept. 10, 1990

It hardly seemed possible that three years had passed since we laid my mother to rest. Widowhood was a lonely road for her with me three hundred miles away in St. Louis, too busy to visit often. The frequency of her visits in my home over the years was a small consolation, yet I feared I had not been the attentive son she deserved.

Leaving Walnut Grove, I began to search for Bud's grave. The unnamed cemetery I sought was a stark contrast to Walnut Grove. Its grass needed mowing. In places, weeds were knee high. Several plots were outlined by six-inch high and six-inch wide concrete borders, most cracked and broken and covered by weeds.

Most of the graves were unmarked, and obviously shallow, judging by row after row of two-by-six-foot unattended mounds. Of the marked graves, more than half the markers were broken and lay on the ground where they had fallen. One large stone had a broken lawn mower blade lying on it.

Some markers indicated the dead to be World War II veterans. It was a surprise to find many World War I veterans buried there. I did not know that any black people had fought in the "Great War."

I had covered half the cemetery to no avail when a little black boy of about ten left his yard and walked over to me. I imagined he was surprised to see a middle-aged white man wandering among the graves of long dead blacks. Curiosity had gotten the better of him.

"Hello, son," I said. "Do you play in this cemetery often?"

"Yes sir," he replied.

"I wonder if you could help me. When you have played here, have you ever seen a gravestone with the name Bud Parrott on it?"

"He'd be over yonder in the white folks' cemetery."

"No, he'd be here. You see he was an old black man who was my friend when I was a boy of about your age."

He did not reply but seemed to drift off slowly in an effort to get away from me. My emotions were about to get the better of me, and I felt I was going to cry.

"I've come a long way looking for his grave," I said. "He meant a lot to me, and I loved him very much. I sure would like to find his grave."

"Wait a minute," he said, "I think I seen him over yonder, here while back."

He began to walk to the northeast corner of the cemetery, and I followed. When we got to where he was going, the grave we found was of someone else entirely.

The little boy said, "I wish I could help you, mister. My grandpa may know. He keeps this place up. He ain't home now, but he'll be home directly."

"Thank you, son, but I think I'll just look around at all the stones until I find him."

The little boy wandered off, and I resumed my search. Throughout the cemetery there were all kinds of debris; pieces of foam containers that long ago held flowers, broken beer bottles and rusted beer cans, pieces of broken granite and concrete were scattered everywhere. I wondered what the little boy's grandfather did to call himself keeping this place up.

Finally I covered all of the cemetery and read every gravestone, standing or broken and lying on the ground. Nowhere was one that said Bud Parrott, or any other Parrott for that matter.

It was midafternoon, and I had spent most of the day in the futile search. I knew he was here; I just didn't know which unmarked shallow grave was his.

I returned to my car and went to my old house. Hungry and tired, I wanted to be in a place he and I had shared. Avoiding the house for now, I went to the area of the property where his room had been. There was the stump of an old mulberry tree that had stood beside the entrance to Bud's room. That tree had served as a step to the roof of the old servants' quarters, one of my childhood escapes.

In the late afternoon sun, fatigue overcame me; and I sat on the ground, leaning back on the stump and fell asleep. Dreams came quickly and in those dreams, it was as if I were out of my body, dying and watching my life go by. I was a young boy again in the back yard in Tuckerman, watching a two-winged World War I Jenny fly slowly by.

I was born in the small town of Tuckerman, ten miles north of Newport, in 1935. All of my people were farmers. Tuckerman was central to the family's farms.

The patriarch of the family was my paternal grandfather, Henry Wood. He was never one to coddle his son, to whom he was a stern taskmaster. Grandpa Henry visited each of his farms daily, making sure each worker carried out his assigned tasks. Even while visiting the farms, Pop, as he was called, always wore a three-piece suit, with a tie tucked into his vest. In one vest pocket was a watch attached by a chain to several keys in a pocket across his chest. His pocket always held a nickel for me. After visiting the farms, Pop spent the rest of each day in his office above Pop Ivy's grocery store, buying and selling real estate or conducting town or school business. He was mayor of the town and president of the school board. Sundays always found Pop at the Methodist Church, followed by a big dinner at home. There, around a big oak table, we would eat fried chicken and listen as Pop picked apart the preacher's sermon.

My parents lived in a house without running water. A hand pump at the kitchen sink meant we were spared running out into the weather to bring water into the house by the bucketful. The unpainted, one-hole privy was out back. Baths were taken in a washtub in the kitchen in the winter and in the back yard at night in the summer.

My father was named Isaac for his grandfather and Henry for his father but was called Ike in his youth and Big Ike later on in life after he became prominent. I was named Isaac Henry Wood, Jr., and naturally was called Little Ike. However, my father was quick to correct anyone who used that nickname for me. He let it be known that folks should call me Isaac, in his book a dignified name. Appearances were important to my father.

My mother, Naomi, was pretty much dominated by my father in apparent contrast to her role in the community. Mother was an avid reader and bridge player. She taught Sunday School, was active in the PTA, and took an active part in community projects such as — during the war years — sewing clothes and knitting socks to be sent to the boys overseas. Most of the vegetables we ate came from her garden. At home, though, Dad ruled. Mom did whatever he said; that was that.

I loved my mother and the times she and I would play cards, just the two of us. Occasionally, she would rub my back after a day of hard play. Rarely, she would let me rub hers after a day of washing, ironing and canning. When she and I were home alone in the evenings, she busied herself needle pointing, sewing or darning socks. She seldom looked up from her tasks to inquire about my games of jacks or military formations of plastic soldiers. While I knew she loved me, Mom never said so. She never hugged me or kissed me, but expressed her love by caring for me, especially when I was sick. My father, on the other hand, scooped me up into his arms each evening when he burst through the door, poking me in the ribs until we both laughed uproariously. When Dad was happy, he read me the adventures of Robin Hood; when he was upset, his footfalls reminded me of the giant in the Jack and the Beanstalk story that Mom had read to me.

About fifty yards north of us lived a black family whose son, Jimmy, was my age. He and I played together almost daily. The first day of school in Tuckerman, I wondered why Jimmy wasn't there. The boy sitting next to me said, "He goes to the nigger school."

That evening I asked my father, "What is a nigger school?"

"Whoa now boy," Dad said sternly. "Don't you ever let me hear you say that word again. It is a very bad word. It's worse than cussing, much worse. It's insulting to colored people. All people are the same whether they are colored or white. Colored people are as good as you and me. I mean it. Don't you ever say that word again!"

Jimmy was my best friend. I didn't think of him as colored. He was just Jimmy.

I will never forget Sunday, December 7, 1941. It started out like any other Sunday: church followed by Sunday dinner at my grandparents' house. Just as the women were carrying steaming bowls of meat and vegetables to the table, the radio came alive with urgent news of Pearl Harbor. I was playing on the floor; my father and grandfather were sitting on the couch. I soon learned where Pearl Harbor was — in the middle of the ocean — and heard Pop cursing the Japanese. Before I understood why a country on the other side of the ocean would bomb us, Pop was cursing President Roosevelt, and saying that it was Roosevelt's war. I remember hoping that I could curse that well when I grew up.

One week later Pop had a heart attack. The next day he died. He had been only fifty-nine; I was six. How could he die? When my father took me onto his lap and told me Pop had died, I thought he was kidding and I laughed. Pop always took me to the farms in his old Chevrolet with the cigarette lighter that turned from green to red when it was ready. He let me ride in a cart pulled by a goat and once even let me try to ride the goat. When I was convinced that it was true, I choked back tears. Pop would want me to be tough. Afterwards, alone in the back yard when nobody was looking, I let the tears come.

My father assumed the role of head of the family — taking control of all the farmland. During the week of Christmas, about three weeks after my grandfather's death, we moved from our tiny four-room house without indoor plumbing to a large house in Newport, the county seat. Newport had fifteen blocks of storefronts and banks, compared to three in Tuckerman.

We moved because our inheritance from Pop's estate allowed us greater comfort, but we also moved for appearances. Soon I came to love our house, with its mysterious dark attic and the large yard, full of oak and maple trees to climb.

There were many kids to play with, and school brought us together. After the small school in Tuckerman, with all twelve grades in one building and only eleven students in the first grade, I was agog at the Walnut Street School in Newport, with only six grades in the entire, two-story building. We set traps of freshly softened bubble gum for the principal to step in and wrote our favorite bad words on the black, slate chalkboard in lemon juice (which we had been assured could not be erased).

Likewise, the streets and alleys of Newport offered many wonderful opportunities for boyhood adventure. Groups of pals made a point to congregate under the long White River bridge to be horrified when big trucks shook its foundation. The musical ice wagon was a veritable magnet on hot summer afternoons. Johnnie MacDonald's tree house was the envy of every kid between short pants and a summer job at Owen's Market. Bag swings suspended from huge oak and pecan trees let us imagine we were Tarzan. Many a summer day was spent sitting on the bank of Lake Newport and fishing for bream with worms and a cane pole.

Life for me was placid until the night, at age eight or nine, when my return home landed me in the middle of a tense scene between my mother and father. During the night, I was awakened by my mother's screams and heard my father cursing and striking her. I was literally scared stiff between my sheets and could not move. Finally, he left in the car, and the house became quiet. Sleep finally came, and the next morning it was as though nothing had happened. Thus, the pattern was set for the next ten years. Liquor, I came to realize, fueled his fits of rage. Until I graduated from high school and left that house, drunken nights and wife abuse became the rule rather than the exception.

By day my father appeared sober as a judge. Nobody questioned his stewardship of family farms and his other businesses. Father was the picture of efficiently. By suppertime he began to drink. It took only a drink or two to launch him into that sphere where only he lived and only he mattered. Mother and I knew we were the likely targets of his fits and his fists.

My first defense was to stay out playing until my mother made me come inside. Sometimes, when the fights began, I would climb out the window and go sleep in the backseat of the family car. When it was too cold outside, I would slip up into the dark attic, wrap up in a blanket and go to sleep on the floor. I doubt I could have made it to age eighteen, when I was to leave for college, had not Bud Parrott come to live with us when I was ten.

Bud had been born in nineteen-two or nineteen-three, he never knew for sure. He was born in a shack in the section of Newport known as the bear pits. He never knew his father. His mother and his grandmother, both of whom took in washing and ironing and occasionally did housework by the day, were his whole family. By the time Bud was four or five, he was running errands for white folks for a penny or two. By the time he was eight, he was chopping cotton in the summer and picking it in the fall. By age ten, he could easily pick a hundred pounds of cotton a day.

Formal education was catch as catch can, but Bud developed reading skills far beyond anything he learned in school. Books were his adventure, his way of escaping the poverty and drudgery of his life. Books made him want to leave and find a better life for himself somewhere else, but he knew he had to stay for the sake of his mother and his grandmother.

His grandmother was a stooped, wrinkled woman who dipped snuff but tried to hide it. When Bud was small, he made a game of staying close to her so she couldn't spit unseen. In spite of the arthritis that curled her fingers and exaggerated the curvature of her spine, she remained a jokester until the winter of 1918. That winter brought with it a strain of flu that proved too much for her. The following summer, Bud's mother married a blacksmith, so he was free to leave.

July and August were the months of cotton chopping in Arkansas; and needing money as he did, Bud could ill-afford to leave then. His plan was to become a hobo and ride the rails to Birmingham, Alabama, where he had read in the *Arkansas Gazette* that the steel mills and coal mines were hiring Negroes and paying well. Knowing how cold an empty boxcar was apt to get in the winter, Bud knew he could not wait to leave until after cotton-picking time in October and early November.

So the decision was made. He would chop cotton in July and August and hop a freight train no later than the first of September. He told no one. His future was his alone. He didn't owe anybody.

On the last Friday of August, Bud decided he had saved enough and it was time to leave. The day was intolerably hot, and Bud could hardly wait for it to end.

All the workers were quiet due to the heat. Bud began to sing.

"What you singin' for, boy?" asked Hillard, whipping his head sideways to get a good look at Bud.

"I'm singin' cause I'm happy that this is the last damn day I ever gonna chop cotton and risk gettin' snake-bit," Bud replied.

"The hell you say," said Sixty, Mr. Hugh Monte's right-hand man. "You gonna die in a goddamn cotton field either a-pickin' or a-choppin' is what you gonna do, and you ain't gonna be a old man when you do it neither."

"Sixty, you are a dumb-ass blue-gum. You ain't got the sense God give a possum," replied Bud.

That led to a fight that destroyed portions of six or seven rows of cotton before it ended with Sixty on his back and Bud standing over him.

"You boys better get up an get outta here 'fore Mr. Hugh Monte sees these here rows of cotton you done knocked over," said Hillard. "Sixty, he gonna have your ass for sure."

Both men got up and all chopped as fast as they could to get away from the destroyed cotton. At dusk, Mr. Hugh Monte McGillicuddy paid Bud, fully expecting him to be back in the field come Monday morning.

Three hours after receiving his last week's cash, Bud went out behind his shack and dug up his coffee can of money. He took the bills and coins back inside and counted out thirty-eight dollars and seventy-two cents.

Into an old toe sack, Bud stuffed two extra pair of bib overalls, two old denim shirts and one nearly new, three changes of underwear, and nine socks. He had no food.

When he stood at the door, Bud turned to look back into the kitchen, barely big enough to contain a white wood cook stove, a rickety table and three chairs, no two the same. The little shack was the only home he knew. Bud didn't want to leave his mama, or even his grandma in her grave.

Closing first the wood door then the screen door, Bud walked down the road to the two-room house his mother shared with the blacksmith. He knocked on the door. The minute his mother pulled the door in, her open mouth and raised eyebrows told Bud that she knew this was likely the last time she would see her son.

"Mama, I gotta go. You know I do. I gotta get away from here and make somethin' of myself."

"I knows you do, baby," his mother said. "I just knows I'll never see you again, and it grieves me."

"You'll see me again, Mama, I swear. I'll come back someday. I just gotta go for now."

"You go, boy, and you be careful and you be happy. Don't forget your Mama, now. And write, boy. I'll get Mother Parks to read your letters to me."

"Have you got somethin' to eat that you can spare?" he asked. "I ain't had nothin' to eat all day."

She went to the cupboard, slapped open a saved paper bag and filled it with six corn pones, a hunk of dried meat and a wedge of apple pie. Mama could not look Bud in the eye when she handed him the food. He heard her husked voice scratch as she said, "God be with you, boy. Now git."

Bud kissed his mother on the cheek. Then he turned into the night and walked toward the Missouri-Pacific railroad tracks. Bud tried hard to take in all the sounds of the night — the crickets, an occasional croak of a frog, the interminable buzz of ever-present mosquitoes, the mournful wail of a far-off train — the sounds of home he wanted to keep in his heart and mind always. He didn't want to leave, but he had to go.

By midnight, a freight train had slowed enough that it could be boarded. Finally, a boxcar passed with the door open; and he ran, threw his poke in first, and then jumped in himself. For a moment he thought he was going to slide back out, for only the top half of his body was inside the car, but with some effort he was able to pull himself inside the dark boxcar.

As the southbound freight began to pick up speed, the clickety-clack of wheels on rails began to slow his racing heart. Soon he began to drift off to sleep. Then he heard, "What you doin' in my boxcar, boy?"

Bud screamed. Then he heard laughter. "Calm down, boy, I ain't gonna hurt you. I'm just a old hobo goin' south like you. We gonna be travelin' companions, so to speak."

As his eyes adjusted to the darkness, Bud was able to make out the form of a thin-bearded white man of indeterminate age. The man's pants had holes in both knees, his shirt seemed to be covering two more of different colors, and his left shoe had a hole from which a toe protruded. Bending forward, the man lit a small fire in front of him, and by its light Bud could make out his features. He had a moldy-looking beard down to the third button of his shirt, a bulbous nose and deep set dark eyes twinkling in the light of the small fire.

"You're a little nigger, ain't you, boy? How old are you, 'bout sixteen or seventeen? I bet you're runnin' away from home."

"Yessir, I'm a colored boy and I'm little but I'm tough as nails, and if you call me a nigger again I'm gonna whip your ass all over this here boxcar," Bud replied.

"Now hold your horses, boy. I didn't mean no offense. I been all over this world with colored folks ridin' these here rails. To me, that word don't mean nothin'; but if it bothers you, I won't use it. I sure as hell don't think I'm any better than you or anyone else for that matter."

"I is sixteen or seventeen. I don't know which. I was borned in oh-two or oh-three is all I know," said Bud.

"Damn, a man oughta know his own birthday. How the hell is they gonna know what to put on your tombstone when you die?"

"It won't matter none to me. I'll be deader'n hell, and there ain't likely to be nobody around lookin' for no will, neither."

"Ain't that a fact," replied the old hobo. "What's your name, boy?"

"Bud Parrott. What's your'n?"

"They call me Sunshine Sam. That's my hobo name. I done near 'bout forgot my real name, I been hoboin' so long. You ain't gonna believe this, but my last name is East, and my daddy named me Dawn. Dawn East is my real name and since the dawn breaks in the east and then comes the sunup, I give myself the name Sunshine Sam when I commenced hoboin' about forty years ago."

"That's a pretty name, Mr. Sam, it sure is," said Bud.

"Your'n is pretty, too, Bud Parrott. How'd you come by such a name anyway?"

"I never knowed my daddy. My old granny told me that he was a real talker — could talk anybody outta anything. He sweet talked my mama somethin' fierce, and once't he planted his seed, he flew like a bird. So they named me for a talkin' bird. They called me Buddy at first. Then Bud. So that's how I come to be named Bud Parrott."

The clickety-clack of the train, the warmth of the night and the flickering of the flames of the fire, which Bud now realized was set in a two-pound coffee can, soon caused both travelers' eyelids to become heavy. In no time they were asleep. The sound of metal on metal woke them at dawn. Sam said the freight was pulling into the Mo-Pac classification yard in North Little Rock.

"Come on, Bud," he said. "Here's where we git off and go git us some breakfast."

"I cain't afford no breakfast," replied Bud.

"Hell, boy, we ain't gonna buy it. We're hobos. We're gonna steal it or work for it, but we ain't gonna go hungry. They likely gonna break up this train here anyways, and if them railroad dicks catches us, they'll billy-club the hell out of us. Come on!"

The men jumped out of the slow-moving boxcar as the train entered the yard. Bud followed in Sam's footsteps as they worked their way through a barbed-wire fence and across a weeded field where a group of small houses lined either side of a dirt road.

"See that pile of firewood?" asked Sam. "Them folks probably needs it split and stacked. That'll buy us breakfast."

The sun was well up, and Bud was hungry. Breakfast sounded real appealing to him.

Sam said, "You let me do all the talkin' now, you hear."

Bud nodded.

A large woman with rotten teeth answered the kitchen door when Sam knocked. Her dress was trailing strings and her apron showed marks where she had run fingers across it after chopping something red, maybe berries Bud thought. "What you want?" she growled.

"My friend and me, we'd sure be glad to split and stack that firewood for you, ma'am, in return for some breakfast."

"You'll do, but I ain't servin' no food to no nigger," she replied.

"Well, ma'am, you'll just have to split your own firewood then, 'cause we're a team. What I do, he does and what I gits, he gits,"

The woman looked at Sam and then at Bud and then at the stack of wood. "Okay," she said, "but be quick about it so you can get fed and get gone. I don't want nobody to see me feedin' no nigger."

The men took to their task. Bud picked up the ax and started swinging, and Sam stacked the split wood. Sam was amazed that Bud, no more than five-nine and a hundred fifty pounds, could split each log perfectly with only one swing of the ax.

Soon their job was done, and they were fed eggs, sausage, biscuits and coffee. When they were finished, they rinsed their tin cups and scratched plates at the pump in the yard. Sam knocked on the door.

When the woman answered the door, Sam handed her the dishes and said, "Thank you kindly, ma'am. That was a fine breakfast."

"Get outta here and don't you never come back. I don't want nobody to see no niggers around my place no more," she growled.

"Well, lady," said Sam, in a drawl that accelerated to a screech, "May yur City Jesus give you just what yur black heart deserves!"

"Yeah," Bud yelled, "That goes for me, too!" Both men took off running, pursued only by the dirty fat woman's blue streak of curses.

When Bud and Sam reached the south end of the classification yard, they crawled down under a railroad trestle, found a big oak stump for a backrest and took a nap. When they awoke, the sun was sinking into the western sky.

"Come on, Bud. It's time to find us a ride."

Bud followed Sam as he made his way in and around the various trains being assembled in the classification yard. All the while they had to watch out for the trainmen, who did not take kindly to hobos. Finally, Sam found a boxcar with its door partially open, and the men climbed aboard. Inside were several large crates that were good for hiding behind. When they were securely hidden, Bud offered Sam a corn pone and some dried meat.

After they had eaten, and while it was still light, Sam opened his poke and took out several frayed writing tablets. On each page was a crudely drawn map. On each map was a written description of where Sam had been at that time, what he had seen and what he had done. Bud was amazed at all the places Sam had traveled. He had been all over the Western Hemisphere as well as throughout Europe and North Africa.

Well into the night, by firelight, Sam delighted his young friend with tales of adventure. Finally, as their fire died down, the two men curled up on a bed of straw and went to sleep.

Sometime in the middle of the night they awoke to find the train had stopped. There was no moon, and it was pitch black. After a while Sam said, "As long as this train is stopped I might as well go out and take a crap."

He got up and felt his way to the door of the boxcar and stepped outside. Suddenly there was a scream, and then all was quiet. Bud called out to Sam and then called again, but there was no answer. He stepped out the door and felt for the ground with his hand only to realize the train had stopped on a trestle. Sam must have fallen some distance to the ground. Again he called Sam's name, again no answer.

Bud groped his way on hands and knees until he came to a brace and post. He climbed down a distance of about thirty feet to the ground and found himself in a swamp. He worked his way back to where he thought Sam to be. Bud called Sam's name, but got no answer.

While standing still just looking at the stars, Bud heard a groan. Following the sound, he made his way to Sam. There was no moon and Bud could barely see. Even in the dark, Bud felt blood on Sam's shirt and something like a bone had been pushed through the knee of his right pants leg.

Sam was barely conscious but, with great effort, was able to speak. "That's a hell of a note," he said, "gettin' killed tryin' to take a shit."

"Hush up," said Bud. "You ain't gonna die."

"Yes I am, boy. I'm killed. Get your ass back on that train and get to where you're goin'. Where are you goin', anyways?"

"I'm goin' to Birminham in Alabama to get me a job in the coal mines or the steel mills. I'm gonna make me some money and be somebody," Bud said between sobs.

"Don't you cry, boy. I've had the good life. Done seen everthing there is to see ... Been everwhere ... Don't you never give up your dream, boy, never. ..." Those were Sunshine Sam's last words.

Bud held his friend's body for the longest, and then he remembered his poke with the thirty- eight dollars and his little bit of food. He climbed back up the trestle, entered the boxcar, got all their things and climbed back down to Sam's corpse.

By sunup, Bud had dug a shallow grave, using a piece of a one-by-six board for a shovel. He buried Sam where he died and fashioned a crude cross on which he carved simply, "Dawn East."

Combining his and Sam's possessions was easy. The only things of interest Bud found in Sam's knapsack were a badly faded photograph of a young woman, of whom Sam had never spoken, and a black rubber comb missing only seven tines. Bud took the comb and left the photo by Sam's cross. He also took the old writing tablets full of maps. Then Bud climbed back up on the trestle and began walking southeastward along the tracks, hoping to find another train soon.

Having studied Sam's crude map of Arkansas prior to beginning his walk, Bud figured he was somewhere southeast of Stuttgart in the White River bottoms. It was unbearably hot, and the humidity was stifling. The air taken in with each breath seemed to have a weight — as though it were solid. Soon Bud was soaked with perspiration. His damp clothes began to attract horseflies and deerflies. Incessant, attacking mosquitoes were nothing compared to the sharp pain inflicted by ferocious flies. Bud was soon swollen beyond recognition. He felt weak, nauseated and dizzy. He feared he might die on the levee beside the tracks.

Somehow, Bud reached a watering station. With great effort, he climbed the ladder to the top of the tank and climbed down inside — into the water. The water was tepid, yet refreshing. It protected his body from flies, although mosquitoes continued to feast on his swollen face.

After floating in his liquid haven until the skin on his fingers began to shrivel up, Bud heard the whistle of a train far off to the north. He climbed down from the water tower, gathered his belongings and moved about thirty yards northward up the track so that when the engine stopped under the water tower, he would be far enough back to slip in a boxcar unnoticed.

Much to his dismay, the train was a logging train and had no boxcars but only flatcars loaded with logs. Not knowing when, or if, another southbound train would be coming, Bud climbed aboard a flatcar in the mid-portion of the train and hid, as best he could, among the logs.

Soon the train pulled off the main track onto a spur and entered a sawmill on the north side of the small town of St. Charles. It was late afternoon, and Bud was hot, sore, tired and hungry. He slipped off unnoticed and walked south along the main track far enough to be out of sight of the sawmill. There he sat on a rail and ate what was left of his dried meat and corn pones.

At dusk, he walked into St. Charles and, when it was dark enough, slipped into a chicken coop and stole a nice fat hen. The commotion raised the owner, who ran into the yard and fired a shotgun in the general direction Bud was running.

At the south edge of town, Bud found a well with a hand pump. He picked up a dipper gourd and drew himself several dippers of water. Then Bud walked about three hundred yards into a clump of trees. He built a small fire, plucked and dressed the chicken, and impaled it's carcass on a green stick for roasting. The chicken meat was tender and warm. It soothed his throat and filled his belly. Bud did his business downwind before returning to the fire to spread out his blanket and settle down for the night. Sleep came quickly.

Shortly after midnight, something awoke Bud. Unsure of the source of the noise, Bud gathered his things and began walking along the rail line. He walked south five or six miles to Cross Roads. He wandered around the town in the dark, occasionally arousing a sleeping dog. Finally, he found what he was looking for, the colored section of town.

By dawn, he saw a gnarled old lady tossing the night's excrements from her slop jar into her side yard. Approaching the house, Bud whistled softly so as not to alarm the old lady.

"Missus," he said, "have you got some chores a hungry boy could do for you to get fed somethin' to eat?"

"Why you's just a baby, boy. Where you come from? You ain't from around here, I knows."

"No ma'am. I'm from Newport on the White River. I'm ridin' the rails to Birminham to get me a good payin' job and get outta the cotton fields."

"Baby, white folks ain't never gonna let you outta them cotton fields. You apt to be a field hand all your life," she said.

"Just the same, I gotta try. I wants to make somethin' of myself other'n just skeeter bait."

"You do that, boy, you keep on a-tryin' an maybe you will make it. You just might. Come on in an I'll give you somethin' to eat."

From somewhere the old lady came up with a feast of a breakfast: eggs, cured ham, biscuits, honey and coffee.

"My name is Pearl Greenberry, honey, but you can call me Granny Pearl. What's your name?"

"Bud Parrott."

"What a pretty name — a bird of many colors and one that can talk, too. You say you goin' to Birminham, is you? Well, you got a long way to go on this side the river 'fore you get to where you can cross it. You gotta go clear down into Louisiana, to Tallulah. Then you gotta get on the railroad goin' east and cross the river into Missippi at Vicksburg."

"Well, whatever I gotta do, I'm gonna do; but I aim to get me a good job."

"Baby, when you cross that Missippi River into Missippi you watch your step. Them white folks over there don't like no colored folk much. Oh, they likes they own colored folk, but they don't like no strangers. Some of 'em would just as soon kill you as look at you. Now, I means it, baby. You better do your travelin' at night an your sleepin' in a safe hidin' place in the daytime."

"I'll be careful, Granny Pearl. I sure will," Bud replied.

Granny Pearl fixed Bud some cured ham and biscuits, put them in a bag and gave him a Mason jar full of fresh well water.

Bud thanked her and went on his way, a little scared but determined.

Bud walked ten miles before another train came. He got lucky, though, because that train took him all the way to Elaine before it stopped.

There his luck ran out. As he was crawling out of the boxcar at the Elaine depot, he was spotted by two of the train crew. One beat Bud with a billy club and the other whipped his legs with a chain. They tossed him, bloodied and semi-conscious, into an oily ditch to die.

When Bud came to, it was early evening, and he was aware that he was not alone. A black man, maybe in his midthirties, was bending over him.

"You alive? Well let me help you up. We gotta get you outta here."

"Who are you?" asked Bud, sounding squeaky to himself.

"My name is Robert Lee Hill, but everbody calls me Bobby. I'm a sharecropper on forty acres over near Hoop Spur Church. Come on, I gotta get you over to my shack and get you cleaned up."

Bobby Hill helped Bud climb up on a bareback mule. Bud sat astraddle the mule, lay his head down on the mane and wrapped his arms around the mule's neck. Bobby led the mule into the darkness, away from the town, down an old dirt road. Bud figured they'd gone several miles. They veered off the road onto a path where Kudzu hung so close on both sides that it scraped both of Bud's shoulders at the same time. Then they were going through a cotton field. Bobby stopped at a small dog-trot shack, telling Bud they were about a hundred yards off the road.

They were met at the porch steps by a once-lovely woman, whose thin face was now framed by white hair. Bud remembered his mama telling of ladies who looked older than their age due to too many children, too many years in the fields and too little help from the men folk.

"Come here and help me, Claudie Belle, I've got a bad hurt young man here," said Bobby.

"Lawdy-Lawd, what in the name of Heaven happened to you, boy?" asked the woman.

"He was ridin' the rails and got caught at the depot. Those trainmen near 'bout beat him to death. Come on, baby, let's get him in the house."

The couple assisted Bud inside, washed him with well water and lye soap. Satisfied he was clean, they laid him out on the dinner table. Several sets of eyes peered over the edge of the table into his face. The children of the house didn't intend to miss anything.

"Brother, go pull me four or five hairs off'n that old mule's mane," Claudie Belle instructed the oldest boy.

"What's your name, boy?" she asked Bud.

"Bud Parrott," he replied through swollen lips.

"Well, Bud Parrott, you better be tough and hold still 'cause I'm gonna have to sew about a foot of your scalp back on."

When Brother came back, Claudie Bell dipped the mule hairs in a black pan of water she had boiling on an old Franklin stove. She then took out one of the hairs and threaded it through a long curved needle. She had Bobby hold a kerosene lantern over her left shoulder and, without so much as a word, began sewing Bud's scalp — beginning at one end and running the stitches in an interlocking fashion to the other end.

Bud bit his lip, he wanted to cry out so bad; but he stifled that impulse and lay perfectly still until she was finished. The entire procedure took no more than four or five minutes.

"You are one tough little feller, Bud," she said. "I bet my Bobby here woulda hollered somethin' fierce if'n I'd of sewed his scalp back on that-a-way."

Bobby grinned a little and nudged his wife with his elbow. He knew how she liked to tease.

For the next two weeks, Bud was given time to heal. His seven nurses were Claudie and all of her children. Bud smiled broadly each time he received a cup of fresh well water, and one of the seven smiled back. Each day the smiles were a little bigger, until they turned into mutual laughter during the second week of his recuperation.

During the nights of his healing, Bud was curious about the arrival of late night visitors, groups of them — all male and all black. They would talk in hushed tones to Bobby Hill. Sometimes the discussions became animated, but Bud could never make out what was being said. Curious as he was, Bud never asked about the night people. He didn't want to be impolite.

One evening two white men wearing lawyer suits appeared at the door. Bobby's enthusiastic way of greeting the men seemed odd to Bud. The three men sat at the dinner table, where they talked and studied some kind of papers for two hours or more. In the end, Bobby signed some papers while the white men pushed their shoulders back and stuck their big bellies out over their belts. Then the older man put the papers in his satchel, and the two left. Finally, Bud's curiosity got the best of him.

"Bobby, I know it ain't polite to ask," Bud said, "but I gotta know. What in the world is goin' on here?"

"Well, Bud, I'm gonna tell you; but you gotta keep your mouth shut, you hear."

"I ain't gonna say nothin' to nobody," promised Bud.

"Okay. These white landlords around here have been takin' advantage of us coloreds for long enough. They give us forty acres to farm and a tumbled down shack to live in. Then they give us our seed and a mule and a plow, and we farm the land. We gotta buy all our groceries and stuff from the company store, and we gotta buy on credit.

"When we bring in the cotton in the fall, we're lucky to bring in two bales for ever three acres, and if we're real lucky we make a bale a acre. For ever bale we get to keep, the man, he gets two. On top of that, we gotta sell our bales to him. Before he pays us he takes out all the money we owe his store, and he charges us for the seeds he give us and sometimes even rent on these old shacks we live in.

"When he gets done takin' out, we ain't got hardly nothin' left.

"And the field hands got it even worse. They gets a dollar a day for choppin' in the summer and a dollar a day for pickin' in the fall, and that's only if they pick a hundred pounds in a day. If they don't, they don't get nothin'."

"Good God amighty," exclaimed Bud. "That's worse than it is up around Newport where I come from."

"Well, we ain't gonna take it no more," said Bobby. "You heard of Mr. Booker T. Washington. Well, he formed the Negro Business League to help colored folks get better jobs and better pay. Some other colored folks up north copied it and started the Farmers and Laborers Household Union of America.

"That's what we're doin' here, we're startin' a local branch of that union, and those two white men are helpin' us. The old man is Lawyer Ulysses S. Bratton; and the young man is his son, Lawyer O. S. Bratton. They're drawin' up the papers."

"Man, you're fixin' to get yourself killed, is what you're doin'," Bud said softly.

"Maybe so, we'll see. Some of the whites got wind of what we're doin', and they're sayin' we are Communists or Bolsheviks or Socialists. Hell, we don't even know what them things are. We're just poor colored folks who just want a fair shake and, by God, we're gonna get it!"

By the end of September Bud was fully recovered and about ready to move on. He still had his thirty-eight dollars and offered to give the Hills some of it as payment for his keep, but they would have none of it.

The day before Bud was to leave, Bobby said, "Hey, Bud, our union is about ready to make our demands. We're meetin' tonight at the Hoop Spur Church. Why don't you come along?"

"I'd be obliged to come, Bobby," replied Bud.

By the time they reached the church it was dark. No women were in attendance, but about fifty or sixty men were there. As Bobby was calling the meeting to order, shouts were heard from outside.

"Robert Lee Hill, come on out here. You're under arrest," a voice shouted.

"My God, Bobby. It's the sheriff and a posse of men," someone shouted.

"What you want me for, Sheriff?" Bobby yelled out a window. "We ain't done nothin'. We got a right to meet."

"Come on out, you're under arrest for bootleggin'."

"Shit, man, Bobby ain't no bootlegger," another man yelled. "Hell, Claudie Belle won't even let him drink!" That brought laughter inside the church.

Suddenly a shot was fired from somewhere, and then the air was filled with gunfire, most from outside but some from inside the church. One of the white peace officers was shot dead and another was wounded in the shoulder before all the black men had fled the church and escaped.

Bud ran with Bobby and a group of seven or eight others. They fled into the woods around Old Town Lake where they spent the night. Their plans were to work their way on east about two miles into the Mississippi River bottoms, where thick swamp brush would make good cover until things blew over.

In the meantime, a genuine riot was breaking out in and around Elaine. Whites were gunning down blacks on sight; and whatever blacks were armed, were firing back.

By dawn Bud and his friends were well into the wooded bottoms of the Mississippi River. When they stopped to rest, Bobby Hill said, "Bud, this ain't your fight. You got a dream. You better hop a freight and git on outta here 'fore you get killed."

"I needs to stay here and help you out, Bobby. I ain't gonna run."

"Dammit, boy. You ain't got no family. All you got is yourself and your dream. I don't need no help, and I sure as hell don't need to worry about no kid gettin' killed. You wanta do me a favor, you'll get your ass outta here."

Bud knew Bobby was right, so he finally agreed to leave. His poke with his money and his clothes were at the Hill's shack though, so he waited behind in the bottoms all through the day until dark came. Cautiously, Bud made his way back to the house. Claudie Belle and all the children were staying inside. Bud let out a big sigh when he saw them all safe.

"How's Bobby, Bud, is he alright?" Claudie asked when Bud came in.

"He's fine. He and some others is hidin' out in the river bottoms 'til this blows over. He made me leave. I'm gonna get my stuff and hop a train."

"You smart to do that. You a nice boy, Bud Parrott. You go to Birminham and get you a good job and find you a good woman." There were tears in her eyes when Claudie gave him a goodbye hug.

It was about midnight when Bud found the railroad and started walking south down the tracks. The moon was full and suddenly Bud came upon a drunken white man with a shotgun.

"Well lookie here," the man said. "I'm a-gonna get to kill me a little nigger tonight. Hold still boy."

Bud was too frightened to move or to say anything. He just stood there as the man drew a bead on him with his shotgun. Bud began to pray without making a sound.

Suddenly a shot was fired, and Bud thought for sure he was a goner. When he felt no pain, he opened his eyes and looked down at himself, finding no wound. Then he saw the drunken white man lying dead along the tracks.

A young black man Bud had heard called Boo, walked up with a smoking pistol in his hand. "Thought you were done for, didn't you? Well, I saved you this time; but I may not be around next time. Bobby said for you to git, so git!" Bud turned to look at the dead man; when he turned back, Boo was gone.

Within an hour, Bud was on a train, alone in a boxcar, heading south. By sunrise, the train was in Louisiana. It was the first time in his life Bud had even been out of Arkansas.

Much later Bud was to find out that the Elaine riots lasted over a week. He heard that upwards of eight hundred people, mostly blacks, were killed.

Almost six hundred soldiers from Camp Pike in North Little Rock were brought in by train to quell the riot. Soldiers, with the assistance of local whites, hunted down and captured or killed many blacks.

Some whites were arrested, but none were ever brought to trial. Twelve blacks were brought to trial swiftly, convicted, sentenced to death and hanged.

To his life-long dismay, Bud never did find out what happened to Robert Lee Hill.

As Bud rode through Louisiana, he began to feel pangs of home-sickness for the familiarity of Newport and Jackson County. He missed his mother and his departed grandmother. He missed Hillard and Sixty and Mr. Hugh Monte. He had made two new friends so far on his trip and had lost both, one to death and one to God knows what.

By the time his train pulled within sight of Tallulah, he felt a little better and reaffirmed his intention to go on.

When the train slowed enough, Bud jumped out. By looking at the position of the mid-autumn sun, he calculated it was about eight or nine in the morning. His stomach confirmed it was past breakfast time.

As he walked through the dirt streets of Tallulah, he looked for a likely house to hit up for a meal; but all the houses had firewood neatly stacked and already split.

Seeing no obvious prospects for chores, he decided to try his luck at a house at random. At the first house he approached, he was greeted by a very large dog with teeth bared. The dog growled menacingly and crept toward the frightened boy. Bud knew he should show no fear, so he stood his ground.

After what seemed an eternity, but was no more than a minute or two, a middle-aged white lady came out the back door and said, "Fuzzy, you leave that nice boy alone! Get back now!"

The dog dropped his head, put his tail between his legs and walked over and stood behind the lady.

"Thank you, ma'am," said Bud, "I sure thought your dog was gonna have me for breakfast."

"Ah, he's just a big sissy. He wouldn't hurt nobody, but he sure can scare folks off. What you need, boy?"

"Ma'am, I'm powerful hungry. I ain't had nothin' to eat since 'fore daylight yesterday. I'd be right happy to do any chores you need in return for somethin' to eat."

"I don't have no chores to do, but I ain't about to send no hungry child away from my door. Sit down on them steps, and I'll fix you a bite. If you want to wash first you can use that pump by the trough," the lady said.

"Thank you, ma'am. I'm obliged to you."

After washing, Bud dried his hands on his shirttail and sat down on the porch steps. Fuzzy, the big dog, lay down at his feet. In a moment the lady returned with eggs, bacon, biscuits and fresh milk. She gave him the food and then sat down on a stump and watched him eat.

"My name is Mrs. Roberts, son. What's yours?"

"Bud Parrott."

"Where you come from, Bud Parrott?"

"I come from Newport up in Northeast Arkansas, ma'am. I been there all my life."

"Wow," Mrs. Roberts exclaimed. "You've come a long way! Where you headed? Are you ridin' the rails?"

"Yes ma'am, I'm hoboin'. I'm goin' to Birminham in Alabama to get me a job in the coal mines or the steel mills. I wants to make somethin' of myself."

"You listen to me, boy. Don't you dare hop a freight an' try to cross that Missippi River on it. Them trains crosses that bridge real slow, and them trainmen likes to catch hobos while the train is on the bridge. They throws 'em off'n the train and off'n the bridge to boot.

It's a long way to the water, and if the fall don't kill'em they'll surely drown."

"Well how'm I gonna get across that river then, ma'am? I gotta cross it somewheres if I'm to get to Birminham."

"Come on, Bud. You come with me. I know a way you can get across."

Bud rinsed his cup and plate, placed them neatly on the doorsill and got up and followed Mrs. Roberts down the dirt street to a blacksmith shop about a quarter of a mile away.

"Dewey," she said, as she approached the blacksmith, "This here is Bud Parrott. Bud, this is my husband, Dewey Roberts."

"How do, Mr. Roberts," said Bud.

Dewey said nothing but just looked at the pair.

"Dewey, you ain't gonna believe this, but Bud is from Newport, Arkansas."

"Well I'll be double-damned," said Dewey, his face lighting up. "I was born and raised in Tuckerman, boy. Damn, it's good to see somebody from home. What you doin' way off down here?"

"He's a-ridin' the rails to Birminham to get a job in the mines or the steel mills," Vera Roberts answered for him.

"You stay outta them mines, boy," said Dewey. "You can get your ass killed in them mines. You be a miner an' you won't live to be no old man."

"That ain't his main problem right now, Dewey. His most pressin' problem is gettin' across the Missippi. You got some wagons and teams to take over to Vicksburg tomorrow, ain't you? Maybe he can ride with you."

"Ride, hell. I got three wagons an' eighteen fresh shod mules. Mose gonna drive one team an' me the other. If'n you can drive a six-mule team, boy, you got a ride."

"Sure I can handle a team, Mr. Roberts. 'Course I ain't never done it before, but you show me how an' I'll do it," Bud replied.

"Ain't nothin' to it, Bud. We'll practice this afternoon. You'll be a real teamster tomorrow. You hang around the shop with me the rest of the day. Vera'll feed you, an' you an' me'll shoot the shit about all them Jackson County folks I used to know."

Bud had two more fine meals that day before and after becoming a teamster that afternoon. The rest of the time he brought Dewey up to date on the goings on in Jackson County while the blacksmith shod the rest of the mules.

That night Bud slept on a straw pallet in the blacksmith shop. Vera brought breakfast to the shop the next morning; and Bud was joined by Mose, a gray-headed old colored deaf-mute, for the meal.

"Mose is deaf and dumb, Bud. He can sign real good, but unless you can sign there ain't no way you can talk to him," Vera explained.

"No'm, I cain't sign," said Bud.

"Too bad. Oh well, that's the way things goes I guess," she replied.

After breakfast, Dewey and Mose hitched the three teams to the wagons. To two of the wagons they tied saddle horses for their trip back home.

"You take the middle wagon, Bud. I'll lead the way, and Mose'll bring up the rear."

As they pulled out and headed down the road, Vera called out to them, "Y'all be careful now; an' Bud Parrott, you take care of yourself now and be a good boy, you hear."

The trip was uneventful, and by midmorning they approached the bridge across the Mississippi River. Bud was astounded at the sight. Never had he dreamed a river could be so wide. He figured it must be a mile across it.

The bridge was a suspension bridge with a railroad in the middle and wooden-slatted roadbeds on either side for wagon or motorcar or horseback traffic. The mules didn't seem to mind the bridge, but Bud wasn't so sure about how he felt. He thought about being thrown from a train off this bridge, and he was even more thankful for the kindness of Dewey and Vera.

Once across the river they headed south from Vicksburg down a road atop the levee for about a mile until they came to a large cotton plantation. Dewey delivered the teams and wagons, was paid and bid goodbye.

He mounted one of the saddle horses, and Mose mounted the other. Bud rode double with Mose back to Vicksburg. At the edge of town, they dismounted and ate the lunch Vera had packed for them.

After they finished their meal, Dewey said, "You're a good hand, Bud. If you want, you can stay in Tallulah an' work for me. I'd pay you a dollar a week and give you room and board."

"Thank you, Mr. Roberts, but I got me a dream. I better keep on goin' 'til I get to Birminham an' get me a good payin' job."

"Okay, Bud, I understand. Hell, I was young once't myself. Here's a half-a-dollar. Now you better be damn careful in Missippi. Some of them folks sure don't like strange colored folks. You better travel by night an' stay hid by day. An' you 'member what I told you 'bout them damn coal mines, you hear."

"Yessir, I'll be careful. An' thank you an' Miss Vera for your kindness. You some of the nicest white folks I ever met."

Bud waved goodbye and watched the two men ride westward until they were out of sight. Then he turned away, a little sadly, and began to walk to the east. Before long he found the railroad high atop a very long trestle. He found a shady dry spot under the trestle, stretched out to rest and waited for the night and a train.

It was well after midnight when Bud finally heard a train approaching. The mosquitoes were terrible, and Bud was afraid a train never would come. He grabbed up his possessions, climbed up onto the trestle and ran as fast as he could to the eastern end of it, where he stepped off onto the levee to await the train.

Before long the train arrived and, luckily, it was going slow enough to be boarded. About halfway down the train Bud found a boxcar with an open door. He jumped in.

"Anybody here?" he asked to the darkened car. No answer. He was alone.

The train moved very slowly, and by four o'clock Bud saw the lights of a very large town. He pulled out Sam's note tablets and found his map of Vicksburg and surrounding parts. The map told him he was approaching Jackson.

Bud decided to stay aboard the train and to disembark only when the train seemed about to stop. To his surprise, the train kept going clear through Jackson.

About a mile east of Jackson in some woods about a quarter-mile from the tracks, Bud saw the lights of what he took to be a hobo jungle. Sam had told him about such places and had assured him that he would always be welcome and would always find food there.

He decided to try his luck, so he jumped off the train and walked toward the fires. When he arrived, dawn was just beginning to break. There were about twenty or thirty men sitting around five or six fires. Most of the men were white, but five or six were black.

As Bud approached the first fire a bearded white man said, "Come on in, friend, an' sit awhile. Get close to the fire to keep away from the skeeters. My name is Homer the Roamer; what's your'n?"

"Bud Parrott."

"Well sit down, Bud. The stew's about ready."

The aroma of the stew reminded Bud how hungry he was. He

smelled carrots, onions and more good stuff. Around the fire sat
Homer and three other men, a black man and two white men.

Homer said, "The colored man is Big Ned."

"How do, boy," said Big Ned.

"How do," replied Bud.

"Them other two is sorta strange. The tall skinny one is called the
Preacher and the other'n is called Walleyed Willie."

Bud looked closer and noticed that Willie's eyes diverged so that
each pointed out away from the other. He could walk down a hall and
see both walls at once.

"Hi, Mr. Willie," said Bud.

"How do, Mr. Parrott," said Willie. That was the first time in his
life Bud was called Mr. Parrott.

"Blaspheme the Holy Ghost," said the Preacher.

"What did you say? What did he say?" asked Bud.

"Blaspheme the Holy Ghost," repeated the Preacher.

"That's all he can say," said Homer the Roamer. "We ain't never
heard him say another word."

"Yeah," said Big Ned.

"Yeah," said Willie.

"Well, boys, the stew's ready. Get out your bowls," ordered Homer.
All three of the others pulled tin bowls and spoons out of their pokes.

"I don't have no dishes," said Bud.

"I got some extry," said Big Ned. "Here, you can keep these." He
gave Bud a tin bowl, cup and spoon.

"Blaspheme the Holy Ghost," said the Preacher.

Bud moved as far away from the Preacher as he could, and Homer
filled his bowl.

"You don't need to be scared of him, Bud, he's harmless. He ain't
gonna hurt you," said Big Ned.

"It ain't him I'm scared of," said Bud, "I just don't wanta be sittin' beside him when the lightnin' strikes him dead."

"Blaspheme the Holy Ghost."

"What's the matter with that man?" asked Bud.

"He's crazy, that's what," said Willie. "He waren't always like that. He used to be a Baptist preacher over in Shreveport. One day he got caught with one of the ladies of the choir. Her husband beat the hell out of him. Then they tarred and feathered him and carried him outta town on a rail. There he was buck-naked an' all an' covered with tar an' feathers.

"I had knowed him before. I'd been hoboin' off an' on, an' he'd fed me a time or two. So when I come up on him I fetched him some clothes an' cleaned him up an' got the clothes on him.

"All he'd say was, 'Blaspheme the Holy Ghost.' That's all I ever heard him say from that day to this'n, an' I've had him with me ever since."

"Blaspheme the Holy Ghost," said the Preacher.

"Damn," said Bud.

After they finished eating Bud cleaned his utensils and placed them in his poke, again thanking Big Ned.

"I gotta be goin'," said Bud. And he got up and started walking toward the east.

"Wait up, I'm a-goin' with you," said Big Ned, and he got up and walked beside Bud.

"Bye, boys; be careful," said Homer.

"Goodbye," said Walleyed Willie.

"Blaspheme the Holy Ghost," said the Preacher.

Big Ned was a large man who Bud figured to be at least sixty. An arthritic gait and a bald pate — except for a semi-circle of gray hair that met above his ears — meant he was past middle age. His eyes were widespread and sad, his nose broad with large flaring nostrils, and his thick lips turned upward in a faint permanent smile contradicting the sadness in his eyes.

The men reached the railroad tracks as the sun read nine, maybe ten. Bud said, "Big Ned, some white folks over in Tallulah told me I better hide in the daytime and travel at night in Missippi. They said those Missippi white folks is terrible mean to strange colored folks. What'd you think about that?"

"Them folks give you some damn good advice is what I think. What you said about lightnin' strikin' that preacher got me to thinkin' I better git goin, even if'n it is daytime," Big Ned replied.

"Maybe we better find us a hidin' place 'fore too long then," suggested Bud.

"Yeah, that's what we better do."

The men walked east along the tracks until they approached a small town. A sign beside the tracks said "Brandon Junction." Off to the south they saw several abandoned sharecropper shacks. They reached the nearest one just as it began to rain.

Bud and Big Ned pulled an old worn-out mattress into a dry corner, and nested into it. Then they sat their cups outside on a stump to catch rainwater to drink.

Rain and a light breeze raised goose bumps on their arms. Bud glanced at Big Ned with a look that said, "I sure wish we could light a warming fire," but both men knew they dared not start a fire for fear of drawing unwanted attention. They lay down on the mattress and covered themselves with their dirty laundry. Lying back-to-back for warmth, they fell asleep.

By midafternoon the rain had stopped. They drank their cups of rainwater and waited for night to come.

"Do folks ever call you 'nigger,' Big Ned?" asked Bud. "It sure makes my blood high when they insultin' me that way."

"They ain't insultin', boy. Lots of Southern white folks cain't pronounce Negro so they says nigger. Anyways, it's how a body says it instead of what they says. If somebody called me a damned nigger, I'd likely take offense. Anyways, I been all over this here country. It's been my experience that white folks in the South hates the race and loves the man, and them in the North loves the race and hates the man. That's why I'm a-stayin in the South from now on out."

By dusk, the men gathered their things and walked back to the railroad. It was good and dark by the time they heard their first eastbound train, but it was a passenger train and was going too fast to board anyway.

Soon they reached a watering station and decided to wait there for a train to stop for water. They hid in some bushes about twenty yards west of the water tank.

About midnight an eastbound freight train approached, and they could tell by the sound it was slowing to stop. Once the train stopped they saw an open boxcar, and Bud got up to go and board it.

"Wait a minute, Bud. We ain't gonna board 'til that train starts up," said Big Ned.

"Why not?"

"Cause them trainmen may check all them cars while they's stopped. We sure don't want 'em to catch us inside."

Sure enough, a burly white man soon appeared walking down the tracks and shining his lantern in all the open cars. Then he closed the boxcar doors. Soon a whistle sent the man hurrying back to the engine.

"Come on," said Big Ned; and the two men ran for the train, opened a boxcar and lunged in.

Big Ned gathered a handful of straw and started a little fire, which he kept burning with bits of wooden slats pulled off crates.

After they got comfortable, Bud asked, "Big Ned, how come you hoboin'?"

"I lived all my life over in Georgia in the Chattahoochee River bottoms near a little town called Blakely. I sharecropped cotton and peanuts. Me and my wife Hattie Mae raised seven churren; had us a pretty good life. Then about ten year ago, my Hattie Mae died. All my churren was growed up and on their own, and nary one of 'em ever seen the inside of no jail.

"I decided then and there I was gonna see the world, so I lit out. I been hoboin' ever since."

"Where all you been?" asked Bud.

"I been all over the United States and into Mexico, but I didn't like it none down there."

"I met a old hobo name of Sunshine Sam back in Arkansas when I started this trip," said Bud. "He been near 'bout all over the world."

"I know Sam," said Big Ned. "We traveled about three months together three or four year ago. We got throwed off'n a train once in the dead of winter near Priest River, Idaho.

"They throwed us out in snow clear up to our ass. We had to walk the tracks two miles into Priest River. Near 'bout froze to death. Sam's toes got frost-bit, and a old sawbones had to cut four of his toes off. I left him there and headed for warmer places. I never seen old Sam no more."

"Naw, and you won't see him no more, neither. He went outta the boxcar, one dark night, to take a dump. The train was stopped up on a trestle. Sam fell off and got killed. The last thing he said to me was it was a hell of a note to get killed tryin' to take a shit."

"That sounds like Sam," said Big Ned, "Damn, I hate he got killed. He was a good 'un."

"He sure was."

The two rode in silence for a long time, and then Bud spoke up and asked, "Where you headin' now, Big Ned?"

"I'm goin' home, boy. I'm fifty year old; feels seventy. I been all over. Learned that one place is 'bout as good as another'n, and one place is as bad as another'n too.

"I ain't seen my churren in ten years. I goin'home to see all my churren and all my grands and stop all this travelin' around. I bet they's a bunch of grands I don't even know I got."

The screech of the train braking for a stop woke them. It was morning, so the two men grabbed their pokes, jumped off the train and ran into the woods.

After the train left, they came out of the woods and walked east along the tracks. Soon they came to a sign that said "Demopolis Junction."

"You can breathe easier now, Bud," said Big Ned. "We's outta Missippi and in Alabama. We ain't much better off here, though. There's some mighty bad white folks in Alabama, too."

"We better be careful then," said Bud.

"Naw, you better be careful, 'cause this is where we part. You goin' to Birminham, and I'm a-goin to south Georgia. You keep on a-goin' northeast, and you cain't miss Birminham. But you be careful now, you hear."

"I'll be careful," said Bud. "So long, Big Ned."

"So long, Bud."

The men began walking in opposite directions. When he got about thirty yards down the track, Bud stopped and yelled, "Hey, Big Ned!"

Ned turned and looked back as Bud yelled, "Blaspheme the Holy Ghost!"

"Shit," said Big Ned as he turned and walked away, laughing.

As he walked northward along the tracks, Bud felt more alone than ever. Here he was in part of the country totally strange to him. He knew no one. Always before he had at least one or two people he could turn to for conversation or advice. He thought how much he would like to have old Sixty or Hillard or Utah or some of his other Jackson County friends to visit with now. He wished Big Ned could have gone on with him.

By noon, Bud's stomach was growling. Having no prospects for a meal, he decided to take a chance and hop a train in the daylight. At the first watering station he found, he helped himself to a big drink of water and then hid to wait for a train.

Within an hour a freight train stopped, and Bud climbed up into a welcoming, open boxcar. He gathered some straw behind three large crates and fell asleep.

It was dusk when he awoke. The train had stopped, and he heard some sort of disturbance outside. He was about to get up when he heard a gruff voice at the door of the boxcar.

"I know you're in there, you son of a bitch. You better get your ass outta there right now, 'cause if'n I have to come in after you I'm a-gonna beat the hell outta you with my billy club."

Bud was very scared, but he dared not move. He tried not to even breathe.

"All right," the voice said. "I'm a-comin' in!""Hey, Harvey," came a voice from down the train. I caught me a ride stealer. Come on an' help me learn him not to steal no rides on our train no more."

"Hold on to him. I'm a-comin," and he closed and latched the door to Bud's boxcar.

Bud waited until the train began to move before he got up and tried the door. Each door was firmly latched from the outside, trapping Bud in the dark car. He groped his way back to where he had been sleeping, gathered the straw into a pile in the corner of the car and set fire to it. He then went to the other end of the car to wait for the fire to burn an opening through which he could escape. All the fire accomplished, however, was to fill the car with smoke. He was choking and coughing, but by the light of the fire, he noticed a trap door in the roof of the car. Bud made a stairway of stacked crates under the trap door, climbed up them and opened the door.

Smoke poured out through the open trap door as though it were a chimney, and Bud crawled out through the smoke onto the roof of the car.

He lay there for a minute getting his breath until the heat from inside the car became unbearable. He jumped off the moving car into the dark, not knowing where he would land. Luckily, the tracks were on a levee. Bud landed on the side of the levee and rolled down into the cool water of a bar ditch.

As he crawled out of the water and gathered his poke, he watched the train, now about a mile up the tracks. The car he had vacated was engulfed in flames, apparently unnoticed by the crew. Bud regretted destroying the boxcar, but he was sure glad to be alive and beyond the reach of that train crew.

On through the night Bud walked, without seeing another train. Somewhere ahead the burned train would be stopped. Bud decided to leave the railroad and walk north on a narrow dirt road.

At daylight, he walked into a small settlement whose road sign said "Centreville." Bud noticed the spelling and was amused that the townsfolk didn't know how to spell "center."

Crowing roosters said the little town was awakening. Mule-drawn wagons were taking workers to the cotton fields, for the picking season was in full swing. Housewives were emptying their slop jars into the outhouses or ditches. Townsmen were going to their jobs. An ice wagon was beginning its rounds.

Bud noticed a large two-story frame building with a sign in the yard that said "Miss Margaret's Boarding House." He decided to try for breakfast there.

His knock was answered by a short, sandy-haired white lady of about forty. She smiled and said, "What can I do for you, young man?"

"Ma'am, I'm powerful hungry. I ain't et in two days. I'd be proud to do whatever chores you got for somethin' to eat."

"Well, let's us get you somethin' to eat first and then we'll worry about chores. As hungry as you look you wouldn't be no good at chores now, anyhow. Come on in an' sit down at the kitchen table, an' I'll get you somethin'."

"Oh, no'm. I can just sit here on the steps to eat," Bud replied.

"Nonsense! Get yourself on in here, boy. You might as well be comfortable while you eat. It's too chilly to eat outside anyway."

So Bud went in, sat down at the table and was served a feast of a breakfast. While going on with her kitchen chores, Miss Margaret asked, "What's your name, boy, and where you headed?"

"My name's Bud Parrott, ma'am. I'm from Arkansas, an' I'm goin to Birminham to get me a job in the steel mills or the coal mines an' make me some money an' make somethin of myself."

"Well, you ain't got far to go, Bud Parrott. Birmingham's only about fifty or sixty miles from here, as the crow flies. I tell you what … I got a friend who's gonna be takin' a couple of bales of cotton into

Birmingham tomorrow. I'll get him to give you a ride in his wagon.

"You can split an' stack that pile of firewood out yonder in the back yard. That'll get you two more good meals today. Tonight you can sleep in the shed out back. After breakfast tomorrow you can ride to Birmingham with my friend, Elwood."

Bud thanked her and accepted her offer. He was surprised and pleased to have received such kind treatment from a white lady so far from his home. He did as he was told, working fast and efficiently. He enjoyed his dinner and supper and had a good night's sleep in the warmth of the tool shed.

After breakfast the next morning, an elderly white man in a two-mule team wagon loaded with two bales of cotton pulled up to the side of the boarding house. Margaret accompanied Bud out to the wagon.

"Elwood, this here is Bud Parrott," she said. "Bud, this is Elwood. This is a good boy an' a hard worker, Elwood. He won't give you no trouble, an' if you need any help he'll oblige you.

"Now, Bud, you take this letter an' give it to Mr. Johnson at the American Cast Iron Pipe Company in Birmingham. He'll give you a job workin' in his factory. I don't want you workin' in no coal mines."

"Why thank you, ma'am. You're the nicest white lady I ever knowed," replied Bud.

"Aw, shoot," said Margaret. "Y'all get gone now."

As they reached the first turn in the road, Bud turned back and waved; and Miss Margaret waved back.

"She shore is nice," said Bud.

"She shore is," replied Elwood.

The trip to Birmingham took the better part of two days. As thanks to Elwood for giving Bud a ride, Margaret had packed enough food for the two of them.

After riding trains, Bud thought the wagon moved at a crawl. However, he noticed villages became larger as they neared Birmingham. Only occasional glances passed between the two men; very few words were said. They traveled well into the night since the moon was full and clouds were scarce. Each took turns driving the team, and when not driving, each man cat-napped.

By midnight, they pulled off the road into a pasture and slept four or five hours, Elwood under the wagon and Bud on a bale of cotton.

Before daylight, Elwood built a small fire and made a pot of coffee, which he shared with Bud. After a breakfast of cold ham and biscuits, they resumed their trip.

The sun said it was maybe two in the afternoon when Elwood stopped and let Bud off in front of the biggest building Bud had ever seen: American Cast Iron Pipe Company. Watching Elwood's wagon disappear, Bud suddenly felt more alone and frightened than he could ever remember. He had never been this far from home, family and friends. Standing at the factory entrance, he watched an endless parade of men carrying black metal buckets out of the gates. Bud stood there for the longest without entering, until a stern-looking, middle-aged white woman opened the door.

"What you want, boy?" she asked.

"Please ma'am, I'd like to see Mr. Johnson. I got a letter for him from Miss Margaret over at Centreville," Bud replied.

"Well ain't that somethin'. I reckon old Maggie still got the sweets for Mr. Dale Johnson else she wouldn't be writin' him. Well it won't do her no good. He's done took, by crackie."

"Oh no'm! This ain't that kinda letter," said Bud.

"You been readin' Mr. Johnson's letter, boy? He'll have your hide for that!"

Bud's frustration was about to get the best of him when a fiftyish looking balding man came to the door, smiled at Bud and said, "Come on in, son, don't let Matilda here fluster you none. Leave the boy alone, Matilda, and get back to your work. What can I do for you, son?"

"Well sir, my name is Bud Parrott, and I come here all the way from Newport up in Northeast Arkansas lookin' for me a good payin' job. I been a field hand all my life, so I knows how to work hard. Since I was eight or nine I been workin' from can to cain't, and I knows they's somethin' better in this world for me than that.

"I run into Miss Margaret over in Centreville and done some chores for her. She give me this here letter to give to you. She said you might have regular work for me here."

Mr. Johnson took the letter, looked at Bud for a minute or so and then asked, "How old are you, Bud?"

"Sixteen or seventeen, I ain't sure which."

"And you come all this way lookin' for work?"

"Yessir."

Dale Johnson opened the envelope and slowly extracted the letter. A soft smile crossed his face as he read it.

"Old Maggie could charm the balls off a billy goat! She's taken a likin' to you, Bud; and she's a good judge of people. Any boy your age who'd come a thousand miles lookin' for work is my kind of folks. You got a job, boy. Now, you got anywheres to stay?"

"I'm a-thankin' you kindly, Mr. Johnson. I'll work hard for you. Naw sir, I ain't found me no place to stay yet."

"I'll tell you what. I'm gonna put you to work in my stock room. The pipes, joints and other fittins' will come off the lines, and your job is to gather 'em up and put 'em in the bins. You can read, cain't you?"

"Yessir."

"Good. The quarter-inch pipes goes in the quarter-inch bins, and the half-inch pipes goes in the half-inch bins and so on. The various sizes of elbow joints and tee joints and such goes in their appropriate bins. You gonna be runnin' your butt off, but you gotta get 'em in the right places.

"Now, 'bout a quarter mile up this road is Miss Lizzie's boardin' house. You can get room and board there for three dollars a week. That's where all my ball players stays. I'm gonna pay you two dollars a day for six days a week. You can have Sundays off. You be at work at seven in the mornin', and you get off at six at night. If you watch yourself, you can make about fifty a month, and your keep'll only be about twelve or fifteen a month.

"If you don't chase women and drink liquor you can sock back near 'bout thirty or thirty-five a month. How's that sound to you?"

"It sounds just fine, Mr. Johnson. It sounds real fine. I'm much obliged to you."

"One more thing, boy. You play any ball?"

"You mean baseball?" asked Bud.

"What other kinda ball is there, boy? Sure I mean baseball."

"Yessir, I played some back in Jackson County. I played on some colored teams we just made up to play some of them old white country boys. We played in cow pastures, mostly."

"Were you any good?"

"Well, I reckon I was. I played third, short and sometimes second; and I pitched a little, too."

"I got me a colored ball team that plays around here," said Johnson. "All of 'em works here for me. We're pretty good, too.

Sometimes we play teams like the Birminham Black Barons; but mostly we just play other company teams — some colored, some white.

"Come next spring, I'll let you try out; if you're any good, you can be on my team. You get time off from work and still get paid. If you play on Sunday you get to split what we get when we pass the hat. How you like that?"

"Just fine, Mr. Johnson, just fine. I'd sure like to play some ball and on a real team, too. I'd be right proud to play for you."

"All right then," said Johnson, "you just keep your nose clean and give me a day's work for a day's pay, and you'll do fine. But you mess up, and you're out on your ass. You understand?"

"Yessir, I do. I won't mess up, I promise you."

On first arriving in town, Bud had a job, a home and the prospects of becoming a baseball player.

Miss Lizzie was a tiny black woman who appeared to be in her seventies. She was gray-headed, stooped, wrinkled and constantly had a dip of snuff in her mouth. The dip was obvious by the bulge in her lower lip and the characteristic smell of her breath, but no one ever saw her spit.

She told Bud she liked him remembering to say "please" and "thanks." Because he was the youngest of her boarders, she gave him a room close to her parlor. Her rules were emphatic: no women, no whiskey and no profanity. Bud said, "No problem!"

Miss Lizzie reminded Bud of his grandmother. His room was papered with an ivy pattern that reminded Bud of Miss Margaret's dining room back in Centreville. And like Miss Margaret, Miss Lizzie served lots of fresh vegetables and corn bread.

Before he turned back the covers on that first night in his room, Bud crawled under his bed, pulled up a corner of the rug and loosened a board in the floor. As quietly as possible he nailed a tin tobacco box to a floor joist. In it, Bud placed twenty of his remaining dollars inside it. Then he replaced the floorboard and laid the rug back over it. Now he had a cache for his money. After paying Miss Lizzie three dollars in advance, he had another five dollars left for pocket money.

The work at the pipe factory was like a game to Bud: run to the quarter-inch bin, then to the five-eights, then the inch bin. It was like a life-sized puzzle that you played with your whole body, not just one hand. When he wasn't out of breath, Bud listened to workers near him, trying to memorize the jokes that got the most laughs, and making a point to remember stories of Sunday escapades.

Except for Sundays, Bud had few choices but to work, eat and sleep. Most Sundays he slept late, frequently missing breakfast. Some Sundays he slipped into a pew at the Piper African Methodist Episcopal Church. After a feast of a Sunday dinner at Miss Lizzie's, Bud pitched horseshoes, read a dime novel or just loafed around.

He listened to older men tell stories of bad bosses, upset girlfriends and narrow escapes — but he seldom shared his experiences. Maybe in part because Bud told little of his exploits, he developed no really close friends. He heard men call him shy and a loner, but Bud felt a quiet life kept him out of trouble and in a job.

By the spring of 1920, Bud had saved enough of his pay that in order to fit his money into the tobacco can he had to trade in a big fist full of one-dollar bills for five twenties: his cache was a little over a hundred dollars. Bud felt settled in his job, and his home at Miss Lizzie's. He even had a few friends at the Piper AME Church.

One day in early March, Dale Johnson approached him at work and said, "Bud, we're tryin' out for my ball team Sunday. We'll be out in the pasture behind Miss Lizzie's. You're welcome to try out if you wanta."

"I'd sure like to, Mr. Johnson; but I ain't got no glove," replied Bud.

"Don't worry about it none, boy. You a lefty or a righty?"

"I'm right-handed."

"Okay, I'm gonna buy you a glove; and you can pay me back fifty cents a month. In three or four months you'll have it paid off. I'll give you a cap for nothin'."

"You got a deal, Mr. Johnson. I'm much obliged to you."

The next day Bud had his new glove. Each night, for the rest of the week, he rubbed linseed oil into the glove to soften it. By Sunday, the leather was developing a pocket where Bud wanted the ball to fit.

Sunday after dinner Bud went out to the pasture. Twenty other black men congregated there. Dale Johnson called them all together and said, "All right, men, this here is Chester Dupens. He'll be your manager. Me an' him will pick the team, an' he's gonna run it. You'll be paid for playin' so he's your boss man. You be workin' for him the same as for me."

Dupens was a large middle-aged black man with graying hair. His belt twisted on each side before disappearing under his belly. The voice that rolled out of his lungs was deeper than any in the church choir and not nearly so polite. Bud had heard stories about bad sergeants in the army and he figured Dupens must have been one in earlier days.

Most players had nicknames, many earned in dubious ways. Scatter Jones was a pitcher with a wild streak. Steel-arm Davis could pitch forever. Balls Berry earned his nickname by the dance he did the previous summer immediately after being struck in the privates by the wicked hop of a ball off the bat of a player on the Stockholm Pipe and Fitting Company team.

"All right, you bastards," said Dupens. "I'm gonna divide you up into two teams, and we gonna play us a game an' see who the ballplayers is."

Bud was placed at third base and had two chances in the first inning going to his left both times — once for a grounder, which he fielded cleanly and threw out the runner at first. The second play was a dive to his left to catch a liner and end the inning.

When Bud came to bat against Scatter in the first, two men had struck out and two had walked. Bud hit the first pitch sharply down the third base line, bringing in two runners.

It was in the top of the second that Bud was to earn his nickname. Again Bud was at third, and Legs Bowen was the first baseman. The first batter hit a sharp grounder to third, and just as Bud bent over to field the ball it bounced sharply in a large wet cow pattie, splattering Bud all over. Without hesitation, Bud threw the ball to Legs.

Legs caught it, and in so doing, got cow feces in his glove and on his hand. He held the ball with his thumb and forefinger for a second, staring at it. Then he threw the ball to the ground, yelled a profanity and charged at Bud. Everyone but Bud and Legs was laughing uncontrollably.

Bud stood his ground, and a fistfight ensued with both men getting bloody. Bud was the last man standing.

Bud had made the ACIPCO team and earned the nickname, "Cow Pattie Parrott" or just Pattie Parrott for short.

As spring wore on and summer arrived, Bud became friendly with Legs and Balls and Scatter and Steel-arm — although he did not become particularly close friends with any of them.

Games were almost always on Wednesday, Saturday and Sunday afternoons; and the players received their regular pay from the pipe company for their ball playing. Most of the Sunday games were double-headers, and the players were allowed to pass the hat between games and keep all the money they collected.

Most of the time Bud played third base, but sometimes he played second, and occasionally in a pinch he would pitch. He wasn't a fast pitcher, but he was accurate. His curve ball was consistent and his knuckle ball bewildered opposing teams.

An endless procession of ten- to eleven-hour workdays, baseball games and occasionally Sunday morning church: that was Bud's life. Having no time for other activities, Bud had no difficulty with Miss Lizzie's "no women" rule.

The excitement of his new life was lost to tedium. The weeks, months and years soon began to run together.

By 1926 Bud was still sorting pipes and fittings, living at Miss Lizzie's and playing ball for Chester Dupens and the ACIPCO team. By that time Pattie Parrott was a name of considerable local notoriety among those who followed baseball in the Birmingham area.

Professional baseball, the American pastime, was a white man's game. Still, everyone knew that there were remarkable black players on mining company teams or other loosely organized groups. By 1920 Negro baseball, though poorly organized, was flourishing. In that year, a large black ballplayer, somewhat past his prime, by the name of Andrew "Rube" Foster founded the Negro National League. The teams were the St. Louis Giants, Kansas City Monarchs, Chicago American Giants, Dayton Marcos, Detroit Stars, Cuban Stars and Indianapolis ABCs.

At about the same time several strong Southern independent teams formed the Southern Negro League with Atlanta, Jacksonville, Mobile and Birmingham the most notable of the teams. This league could not compare with the Negro National League in stature due to the organizational abilities of Rube Foster, whose Northern teams were allowed to play against whites, whom they frequently defeated.

Every young black ballplayer dreamed of playing for one of the Southern Negro League teams, if not a Negro National League team. Bud was no exception.

One Sunday in April of 1926, Dale Johnson arranged for his ACIPCO team to play an exhibition game against the Birmingham Black Barons of the Southern Negro League. Bud and his teammates were beside themselves with excitement. They were to play a Sunday afternoon game and face the great Leroy "Satchel" Paige, who had just come to Birmingham from Mobile that season.

Although the ACIPCO team lost, Bud had a fabulous day going four for five with a homer and three singles and playing errorless ball in the field.

After the game, Paige and a short fat man in a baseball uniform approached Bud.

"Hey, Parrott," said Satch. "You done pretty good out there today. 'Course, I took pity on you and let you hit the ball. If I'd of really been tryin', you wouldn't of done so good. But you're a pretty fair ballplayer."

"Thank you, Mr. Paige. You sure can pitch that ball. I really got lucky today."

"No you didn't, boy. You're a damn fine ballplayer," said the fat man, "How'd you like to play for me?"

"You mean it? You mean on the Black Barons?" asked Bud excitedly.

"I sure do. I need a third baseman what can hit, an' if'n you can hit old Satchelfoot here, you can hit anybody.

"I'll pay you fifty a month an' pay your room an' board on the road. "Course you'll have to give up your job at ACIPCO, but I betcha old man Johnson will let you work in the off-season for him. Well, how 'bout it?"

"Mister, you done hired you a third baseman," said Bud.

As much as Bud looked forward to being a professional ballplayer, he still hated to leave ACIPCO, for Dale Johnson had been good to him. Even Matilda, Mr. Johnson's secretary, had finally warmed up to the mannerly young black man.

Bud could hardly sleep that Sunday night because of his excitement but also because of his dreading the confrontation with Dale Johnson.

Shortly after he arrived at work the next morning, he went to the office to see Johnson.

"Miss Matilda," he said. "Would you please tell Mr. Johnson I needs to talk to him for a minute?"

"You ain't in no trouble now, are you, Bud?" she teased.

"No'm. It ain't nothin' like that. I just needs to talk to him."

"Well, knock on the door and go on in, boy. He ain't doin' nothin' he cain't stop doin' to talk to his star ballplayer."

When Bud entered the office, Mr. Johnson rose and came around his desk, extending his right hand. "Put her there, boy. You played a helluva game," he said.

Bud shook his hand, thanked him for the compliment, then said, "Mr. Johnson, you been real good to me these past six years. I never had a job I liked better or worked for no nicer man, white or colored.

"But I tell you, Mr. Johnson. The skipper of the Black Barons done offered me a job playin' third base for his team, an' I don't see how I can turn him down."

"You'd be a damn fool to turn him down. Why, you'd likely be famous playin' professional ball. Yeah, an' it'd be a feather in my cap, too, 'cause I done found you and trained you an' taught you to be a ballplayer.

"Why, hell yes, you take him up on the offer, an' in the winter time when you ain't playin' ball you can come back here an' work for me."

Bud was so happy he almost cried. Here was a white man genuinely happy that something good was happening to him.

"You better gather up your stuff, boy, an' take off an' join that team 'fore they change their minds. Damn! I never seen nobody hit Satchel Paige the way you hit him. I thought that homer you hit would never come down.

"Now, Bud, if you ever get off in any of them cities an' get in any trouble or need anything you just call me an' I'll come a-runnin'. You hear me?"

"Yessir, I do, Mr. Johnson. An' I ain't never gonna forget you, neither," replied Bud.

So Bud walked out the door, telling Matilda goodbye, on the way to an adventure he never dreamed possible.

Blackie Pickens, the manager of the Black Barons, was a short man with close-cropped graying hair. Bud figured Blackie was about as wide as he was tall. Blackie was a man of few words, but his voice was deep and sonorous. A man with commanding presence, Mr. Pickens encouraged his players to have fun and put on a show for the fans. He expected a player's best effort when a game was on the line.

Most games were not as serious as league play; most were exhibitions against local amateur teams — sometimes black, sometimes white. The rule of thumb was that local teams were not to be beaten so badly as to embarrass them, but instead to get a comfortable lead and then coast the rest of the game. That way the locals were likely to invite the Black Barons back for another game and another payday.

Most of the team lived at the Rush Hotel, which was owned by the proprietor of the team. Bud, however, continued to live at Miss Lizzie's. When traveling, the team stayed in private homes or slept on the bus or at the ballpark, due to segregation. On the road, Bud, being the only rookie on the team, was assigned to room with Satchel Paige so he could be educated to the ways of the league by the league's star player.

Satchel Paige was long and lanky. His wingspan and size sixteen shoes caught the attention of fans everywhere they went. Although he frequently played the clown and acted dumb, he was actually a quiet, intelligent man. Paige politely declined his teammates' invitations to join them on late-night romps; he preferred a quiet dinner followed by the companionship of a good book and an early appointment with a solo pillow. His teammates didn't know what to think of him. Paige's talent commanded ten to fifteen percent of the gate receipts at most of the exhibition games, a reality his teammates resented. They also resented that he frequently arrived late for games. He might pitch, or not pitch, depending on his mood or the size of the crowd. But he could be humorous, and his love of life was infectious, adding to his teammates' ambivalent feelings toward him.

Bud idolized him and found it hard not to call him "Mr. Paige."

"Pattie," Satch said on one rather long bus ride, "I ain't no older'n you. Now you stop this 'Mr. Paige' stuff an' call me 'Satch.' I mean it."

"Okay, Satch," Bud replied. "How'd you get that name anyway? You called Satchelfoot 'cause of them big feet or what?"

"Naw, back in Mobile when I was redcappin' at the depot I could get three satchels up in under each arm and one in each hand. I could carry eight satchels at a time; so they called me 'Satchel' an' it took. Somebody just made that Satchelfoot thing up. My feets is big but they ain't that big," Satch replied.

"They's big enough for you to write 'fastball' on the sole of your shoe, though."

"Yeah, I done that once't. I wrote it on the bottom of my left foot, so when I kicked it up just 'fore I let fire the ball, the batter'd see it an' get bumfuzzled. Now folks talk like I do it all the time.

"I'll tell 'em a fastball is comin', though, an' dare 'em to hit it. Most of 'em cain't touch it when I put the mustard on it."

The 1926 season ended with Bud playing almost all the games at third base and batting .325. Winter passed uneventfully, and the spring of twenty-seven brought the Black Barons' admission in the Negro National League.

They traveled by train or bus to games in Chicago, Kansas City, St. Louis, Memphis, New York and Cleveland. Between league games and the many and varied exhibition games, the Black Barons played over one hundred fifty games that year. They won the second half of the league season but lost four straight playoff games to the Chicago American Giants to lose the pennant.

Again Bud did well, batting .362 and making very few errors in the field. His season ended on a sad note, however, when his friend and mentor, Satchel Paige, left the Barons for more money with the Cleveland Cubs.

Several other star players left Birmingham for the Cubs with Paige; and even though he played two more years for the Black Barons, baseball in Birmingham was no longer fun for Pattie Parrott, the man who threw a shit-ball to earn his name.

As much as Bud loved baseball, traveling through the South by bus began to become drudgery. The trips were long; and, segregation being what it was, accommodations were modest to non-existent. Only in Birmingham and Miami were there decent hotels for blacks, so lodging was in rooming houses or private homes. Frequently no lodging was available, so the players would sleep in the bus or in the dugout where the next day's game was to be played.

With no black restaurants in many cities, the Barons usually ate on the bus — bologna sandwiches and soda pops. One year the Barons had a third-rate player they hired solely because he could pass for white. It was his job to go into restaurants and order hot dogs and hamburgers to go. Even he failed if the restaurateur spotted the busload of blacks waiting outside.

By the spring of 1931, Bud was ready to give up the insults and hardships that came with black league baseball. Bud had to admit to himself that he was also bored with Birmingham, his job at ACIPCO and his solitary room at Miss Lizzie's. Bud's secret cache now held three hundred twenty-one dollars and fifty-five cents — a small fortune to Bud. Fellow players had heard his mumbling. Hitting the rails with Sam's notebooks was sounding pretty good to Bud.

One evening as Bud approached the gate after work, Blackie

Pickens was standing there waiting for him. Bud was surprised, but not too much.

"Hey, Pattie," Blackie called out.

"How do, Blackie. What you doin' out here?"

"I come to see if what I been hearin' is true. I come to find out if'n you really is goin' to quit on me."

"I done had it with baseball an' Birminham an' my damn borin' job an' the South to boot. I'm tired of not being able to get nothin' decent to eat nor no decent place to sleep," Bud said.

"I figured as much." said Blackie, "Before you take off you better hear what I have to say. Mr. Gus Greenlee, the owner of the Pittsburgh Crawfords, sent you a telegram, care of me. I read it. Seems like old Satch is playin' for him now, and Satch told him you's a player he wants for his third baseman. He's offerin' you a hunnerd an' a quarter a month, an' he'll find you a wintertime job in a steel mill so you can have year-round income.

"You's crazy as hell if'n you don't take his offer. He's a powerful man on the Pittsburgh North Side. An' a hunnerd an' a quarter is damn good money, what with the depression an' all."

It took Bud no time at all to make up his mind. "When I gotta be there?" he asked.

"They playin' their way back to Pittsburgh since they done finished spring trainin'. You got two weeks to get there. You to meet him a week from next Monday in his office, back of the Crawford Bar and Grill. If I was you I'd be there bright an' early that mornin'."

"Send him a telegram for me, will you, Blackie; an' tell him I'll be there. I gotta get my stuff together, get me a train ticket an' get a-goin'," said Bud.

Bud walked into Dale Johnson's office hat in hand, with his chin nearly touching his chest. Mr. Johnson had been kind and encouraging to him, a legacy of kindness Bud knew he could never forget. And Miss Lizzie: Bud told her that she had become a "second Mama" to him, which precipitated tears from her and him, too.

"Baby," she said, "them big city folks up North'll eat you alive. They gonna see you as some dumb little old southern colored boy that ain't got no sense. You better stay down here in the South where folks knows you, an' you knows them."

"Naw, Miss Lizzie. I'll do all right. Satchel Paige is there, an' he knows his way around. He'll teach me all I needs to know."

"I see you done made up your mind, baby. Well, you go on then but be careful. May the Good Lord go with you," she said.

Bud's sleep was interrupted that night, first by a dream of playing on the Crawfords' big field, and then by a nightmare in which all of the people who had been so good to him in Birmingham were sitting in the church choir loft, but out of earshot. He kept calling their names, even with the preacher in the middle of his sermon, but they acted as if he wasn't even there.

Bud remembered his conversation with Mr. Johnson.

"Mr. Johnson, I got me a offer to play for the Pittsburgh Crawfords. Mr. Gus Greenlee wants me there a week from Monday. I don't see how I can turn that offer down."

"Hell no, you cain't turn it down. Hot damn; you done hit the big time, boy. Yes sir, you sure better snap that up."

Bud was relieved that Johnson was so happy for him. "I'll be able to work out the week for you, but I'll need to be leavin' by Sunday if'n that's okay by you."

"Sure it is, Bud. That'll be just fine. It'll give you a few days to show the ropes to whoever I find to take over your job.

"Now you listen to me. One of these days somebody's gonna wake up an' hire some of you colored boys to play in the major leagues. Y'all can play rings around most of them white boys anyhow. You're only twenty-seven. You play your cards right an' it just might be you.

"Then I can tell everbody I taught you all you know!"

So Bud worked out the week and said his goodbyes. Early Monday morning he boarded the train, took a seat in the car for coloreds and started on his journey to Pittsburgh. He remembered riding into Birmingham on a farm wagon ten years earlier and figured leaving on a train meant he was coming up in the world!

The first stop was Atlanta, a hundred sixty miles from Birmingham. The car for coloreds had only seven passengers so Bud just read his Bible.

Remembering his hobo days when traveling companions filled the time with tales of adventure, Bud missed interesting conversation, even though his accommodations were not as comfortable as on this trip. He wondered what had become of Bobby Hill, Big Ned, Homer the Roamer, Walleyed Willie and the Preacher. He was homesick, in a way, for those old friends, though he didn't miss the Preacher's verbal blasts. Bud doubted he would ever see any of his Birmingham friends again, a realization that saddened him. Then he realized that playing for the Crawfords would bring him back to Birmingham to play the Black Barons. Surely his friends would come to see him play. Maybe the Crawfords could play the ACIPCO team in an exhibition game.

Every couple of hours, the train stopped for water and fuel. At an early afternoon watering stop the passengers disembarked to lunch at a cafe by the depot. Black passengers were also allowed to buy lunch, but they were escorted outdoors behind the kitchen to be served on picnic tables.

At Atlanta all passengers left the train. Bud spent the night in the colored waiting room, sleeping on a bench. The next morning he relieved himself at a privy behind the depot and drew water from a well to wash. There was no breakfast.

By midmorning his train left for the one hundred fifty mile trip to Greenville, South Carolina. Over the next three days his train stopped in Charlotte, North Carolina; Roanoke, Virginia; and then to Charleston, West Virginia — where his life was to change forever.

Bud slept in the Charleston depot that Friday night. The Pittsburgh train didn't leave until noon on Saturday, so he wandered the town looking for breakfast. Bud procured coffee and a biscuit at the back door of a café, which also allowed him to use its outhouse. He then returned to the depot and boarded his train.

Shortly before the train pulled out two black women boarded and took seats across the aisle from him. Bud noticed their impeccable posture and their fine dresses. One woman looked to be in her late sixties or early seventies. She was tall and erect. Obviously, she had been very beautiful in her youth, and even now she was handsome.

The other woman was in her early twenties. Bud realized he was staring at the most beautiful woman he'd ever seen. She was about Bud's height and was satisfactorily rounded in the critical places. Her skin resembled pure ebony, her hair was curly and shoulder length, her teeth were straight and as white as ivory and her eyes were dark and mirthful.

Bud could not take his eyes off her, a fact that was soon apparent to both women. The younger woman seemed embarrassed, though mildly amused. The older woman was in no way amused and became obviously quite huffy.

Finally, she looked at Bud and said, "Young man, do you make it a habit to stare at folks on a train?"

"No ma'am, I don't," replied Bud, "an' I know it ain't polite to stare, ma'am; but I just cain't help it. I swear, ma'am, I ain't never seen nobody as pretty as the young lady here."

Bud's candor surprised and amused the old lady. She smiled and said, "Well at least you're honest. Where are you from, young man? You don't talk like you're from around here."

"No'm, I ain't … I'm not. I'm from Arkansas, but I been livin' in Birminham workin' in a pipe factory an' playin' baseball. I'm a professional ball player. I been playin' for the Birminham Black Barons, but I'm on my way to Pittsburgh where I will play for Mr. Gus Greenlee's Pittsburgh Crawfords."

"I love baseball," said the younger woman, a gleam in her eyes. "Granny an' I go see the Crawfords play a lot. We know Mr. Greenlee, too. We live on the North Side close to his cafe."

"What's your name, young man?" asked the older woman.

"Bud Parrott, ma'am."

"Not your nickname, boy, your Christian name," she said.

"That's the only name I got, ma'am. That's what my mama an' my granny named me."

"I see. Well, they didn't give you a decent name; but they taught you manners and seemed to have brought you up right. You go to church?"

"Yes'm. I was brought up in the Beulah Land AME Church in Newport, Arkansas, an' I been goin' to the Piper AME Church in Birminham when I ain't been playin' ball outta town on Sundays."

"You're all right, Bud Parrott. Yes sir, you're all right. My name is Rosalee Jones; and this young lady is my granddaughter, Queen Esther Robinette."

"It's real nice to meet you ladies," said Bud, rising slightly from his seat.

"I just might come watch you play baseball sometime, Mr. Bud Parrott," said Queen Esther.

"If you let me know you're comin', I'll get you good seats an' try my best to hit a homer for you," said Bud.

"You got a deal, Mr. Parrott. An' if you hit me a homer, I'll bet old Granny here'll invite you over to our house for a Sunday dinner."

By the time they reached Pittsburgh late Saturday night, Miss Rosalee was quite smitten with the young gentleman from the South. Though less obvious about it, so was Queen Esther. Realizing Bud had no lodging, the women took him by cab to the Crawford Recreation Center where he was able to get a room for the night.

The next morning, on the advice of the ladies, Bud went to Miss Hattie Blanton's three-story clapboard rooming house on Wylie Avenue and secured a room for five dollars a week. Bud figured the room was nine feet by eleven feet, considerably larger than his room at Miss Lizzie's in Birmingham. It was wallpapered in a wisteria trellis design and furnished with an oak bed, an upholstered chair, and chest of drawers with a white crockery pitcher and bowl on top. An indoor toilet and shower room were nearby.

Miss Hattie's two hundred pounds (at least, Bud figured) were draped in a yellow dress that jiggled all over when her mood turned jovial, which was often. As jolly as she was, she tolerated no monkey business. That night after Bud had settled in he went downstairs and had a long visit with Miss Hattie.

"Bud," she said, "I done told you the rules, an' I 'spect you to foller 'em. No women an' no liquor. I mean that now."

"I know, Miss Hattie, that won't be no problem for me."

"Breakfast is at seven, dinner at noon, an' supper is at six-thirty. You late an' you don't eat."

"Yes'm."

"You got any other questions?" she asked.

"Yes ma'am, I do. What can you tell me about Mr. Greenlee an' the Crawfords?"

"All right, Bud, now you listen good an' you keep this to yourself. At least don't tell nobody I told you nothin'.

"Gus Greenlee is a powerful man an' rich to boot. He runs the numbers racket on the entire North Side."

"Pardon me, ma'am, but what you mean by the numbers racket?" interrupted Bud.

"You bets whatever you want, a penny, a dollar, a hunnerd dollars; an' you picks three numbers. Then you looks in the paper for what the stock market closed at that day, an' the last three numbers is the winnin' numbers. If yours matches 'em, you wins about five or six hunnerd to one. Nobody hardly ever wins.

"Anyways, Gus is powerful an' rich; an' you don't wanta cross him. He owns the Crawford Bar and Grill over on Crawford Avenue. Got good food an' good entertainment.

"He was jealous of the Homestead Grays over 'cross town. He talked to old Cum Posey an' tried to buy the team, but Cum wouldn't sell. So he started up his own team an' hired players like Satchel Paige. He named 'em the Crawford Colored Giants after the Crawford Recreation Center where you stayed last night.

"They say he's put up a hunnerd thousand dollars to build his own stadium, an' it oughta be ready by next year. I'll say one thing for old Gus; his word is his bond. You do right by him, an' he'll do right by you."

Bud thanked Miss Hattie for her advice and information, excused himself and went to his room. Tired as he was, he couldn't sleep. He was excited about starting with his new team and particularly about again having Satch for a teammate. More than that, though, he had reservations, if not outright fears, about getting involved with gamblers. Bud had never been afoul of the law, but he had known men who had, and the consequences they had faced were certainly not pleasant.

He remembered once when Sixty Nine had been arrested and charged with drunk and disorderly back in Newport. The police roughed him up a little when he refused to admit he was an alcoholic. After awhile the policemen told Sixty if he would just admit he was an alcoholic they would leave him alone.

Sixty said, "Listen. I'll take a drink. I'll take a drink any time an' with anybody. I'll take a drink with a cross-eyed gutter drunk an' give him the first swig, but I ain't no al-kee-holic!"

That brought him a severe beating and four days in jail, but he never did admit he was an alcoholic. He wasn't one either; he just liked to celebrate *every* Saturday night.

Finally, Bud decided that he couldn't be held accountable for what his boss did. Satch, Cool Papa and the rest of the Crawfords had no trouble with the law. So he eventually drifted off to sleep, although he slept fitfully the rest of the night.

After breakfast the next morning, Bud walked the two blocks to the Crawford Bar and Grill. The façade was a stunning blue and white checkerboard, made up of tiles that almost glowed in the morning sun. Bud figured a bunch of numbers money went into those shiny tiles. Inside, along the left wall was a long bar of the fanciest quarter-sawn oak Bud had ever seen. Below were a polished brass rail and spittoons. Behind the bar was the kitchen, which had a large double oven and the largest grill Bud had ever seen. On the wall opposite the bar were nine booths, each designed to seat four, except for the front and rear corner booths, which had room for six.

Upstairs was a large dance hall with a raised bandstand at the far end. Behind the bandstand was Gus Greenlee's office.

When Bud entered, the bar was empty except for an old gnarled black man who was washing dishes.

"Beg pardon, mister," said Bud, "but could you tell me where I could find Mr. Gus Greenlee?"

"Yeah," the old man said without looking up.

There was a pause, and then Bud said, "Well, will you tell me where he's at?"

"Who wants to know, godammit?"

Bud didn't know what to make of the old man.

"I do," he said. His voice tremulous.

The old man looked up. "Well, just who in the hell is you?"

"My name is Bud Parrott, an' I'm a ballplayer."

The old man's face lit up, and he said, "Yeah, I heard tell of you. You the boy that throws the shit-ball, ain'tcha?"

"I reckon I am all right. I don't guess I'll ever live that down."

"Hell naw you won't, but you oughter be proud of it. You thowed the guy out, didn't you? That's the name of the game, boy. You don't never let nothin' get in your way of makin' a play, least of all a little shit. Go up them stairs an' through the door to the left of the stage. That's Gus' office. He be a-waitin' for you. Yessir, we got us a real shit-thower!"

Bud did as he was told and when he knocked on the door, a deep voice ordered him to come in. Greenlee rose and came around from behind a dark desk Bud figured was the size of three coffins, and a whole lot prettier than anything ever put in the ground back in Newport, Arkansas. Greenlee extended a bony hand attached to a hairy arm and greeted Bud with twenty shakes. The man was not what Bud had imagined. He was slender, of average height and about forty or forty-five. He wore an expensive dark double-breasted suit, black and white wingtip shoes and his hair was neatly combed. A thin well-trimmed mustache danced above a large gold tooth.

"It's good to have you here, boy. Satchel Paige tells me you're a fine ballplayer. With Satch on the mound, Cool Papa Bell in center an' now you on third I got me the makin's of a real team. I'm gonna get Josh Gibson to catch for me next year when he's free to move. His boss don't know that yet so you cain't say nothin' to nobody about it. Yessir, we gonna have us *a team*."

"I sure am proud to be here, Mr. Greenlee. I ain't never lived in the North before, but I betcha I like it. It'll sure be good to see old Satch again, too."

"Now Bud, you gonna need a job in the winter. You look like a honest boy to me. How'd you like to be a numbers runner for me?"

"Thank you, Mr. Greenlee, but if it's just the same with you I'd rather not take no chances with the law. My boss at the pipe company down in Birminham told me about a friend of his'n at a steel mill here who would hire me in the wintertime. I think I'll give that a try."

"That's fine with me, boy; but that's sure 'nuff hard work. Hotter'n seven shades of hell, too; but if that's what you want, then go to it. There ain't no laws gonna mess with the numbers, though. I got 'em all paid off; an', anyways, everbody plays the numbers an' the law don't give us no second thought."

"Well thanks just the same, but I'm gonna give the steel mill a shot when the ball season's over."

"You stayin' over at Miss Hattie's, I hear. That's good. Be at the Recreation Center tomorrow at two o'clock. We practice then. My man Woogie, he'll have you fixed up with everthing you'll need.

"Yessir, we gonna have us a helluva team. We're gonna beat them Grays up one side and down the 'nother."

🦗 🦗 🦗 🦗

At the Crawford Recreation Center the next afternoon, Bud was greeted by a frenetic little man, who seemed to be everywhere at once. Woogie was Gus' right hand man and essentially ran the team for him.

Bud suited up and soon was greeted by the rest of the team, many of whom he already knew. There was Satchel Paige, of course, and Cool Papa Bell, Oscar Charleston, Ted Page and Judy Johnson, all of whom were already stars and nationally known.

Practice went well, and Bud fit right in. His nickname and the notoriety of the shit-ball had preceded him so he took a lot of good-natured kidding.

The next two weeks were an established routine: practice seven hours during the daylight and party seven hours after dark. After the first three nights of standing like a drugstore Indian during the after-dark part of the schedule, Bud decided to stay home and read or just wander around the neighborhood.

The next Sunday he walked twelve blocks to the Greater St. Paul AME Church on Wylie Avenue, following directions Miss Rosalee gave when she and Queen Esther dropped him off earlier. Before entering the church through wide double doors, Bud noticed the name of the pastor on the sign out front. The name was The Reverend Robert Robinette, and Bud couldn't help but wonder if he was related to Queen Esther.

From the front row, Miss Rosalee motioned for Bud to come down front and sit by her. Bud, accustomed to sitting as far from the Pastor's thunder as possible, didn't want to offend Miss Rosalee, so he did as she wished.

When the robed choir entered, Bud could not help noticing that the third robe from the left in the front row was filled very nicely by

Queen Esther. Queen Esther smiled when she saw Bud. He thought
he saw her wink at him.

Bud leaned over and whispered in Rosalee's ear, "Is Reverend
Robinette ..."

"He be her daddy. He's my son-in-law. My daughter, Queenie's
mother, is long dead. Me an' the Reverend raised Queenie, an' we
done a fine job of it too."

"I'll say!" said Bud, causing Rosalee to smile and then stifle a
laugh.

When the Reverend Robinette appeared, Bud could see where
Queen Esther got her looks. He was a large, muscular, very dark man
of about fifty and was the most handsome and most impressive man
Bud had ever seen. His voice was a booming bass, his diction precise
and his grammar perfect.

Reverend Robinette talked temptation, sin, perdition and damna-
tion. Before the sermon ended, Bud was sure he was going to Hell.

After the service Reverend Bob, as he was called, stood at the
narthex and greeted the congregation one by one as they filed out into
the sunshine. When Bud approached him, Rosalee said, "Bob, this
is Bud Parrott. He's the ballplayer from the South we told you about
meetin' on the train. He's sweet on your daughter, I think."

It was all Bud could do to remain standing. He didn't know what
to say or do. He just stood before the magnificent Reverend unable to
make anything intelligible issue from his gaping mouth.

The preacher just rolled his head back and laughed heartily.
"Don't let old Granny get your goat, Bud. She's just a big tease. You'll
come to the Parsonage for Sunday dinner, won't you? The least
Granny can do is feed you after embarrassing you so."

"Thank you very much, Reverend. I'll be pleased to have dinner
with you and your family."

So Bud went to Sunday dinner at Queen Esther's house.

After that Sunday Bud attended Greater St. Paul's every Sunday his baseball schedule would allow. Before long he had a standing invitation for Sunday dinner as well.

Bud and the Crawfords prospered. By midsummer, their league record was five wins and seven losses. They had won all their exhibition games against semi-pro and amateur teams.

The addition of Judy Johnson, an established third baseman, created a problem that was soon solved with Bud moving to second base. Much to his surprise Bud liked second better than third. For one thing, the throw to first was easier. Also, he liked having more ground to cover at second. Mostly, however, he liked being away from the home dugout on road trips and thus not having to hear taunts and jibes about his shit-ball.

By midsummer Bud had also contacted one of the small steel mills that made and supplied steel billets to large mills such as U. S. Steel. He was promised a job in the melting room during the off-season.

Most of the better ballplayers had been offered jobs playing in Mexico, Cuba or the Dominican Republic in the Winter League. Bud turned down a nice offer to go with them, saying that he needed to get established in a job he could work at after he was too old for baseball. Satch, Cool Papa and the rest knew that the real reason he wanted to stay in Pittsburgh during the winter was Queen Esther, and they teased him unmercifully about it.

The first Wednesday in August, Bud left his afternoon ball game early, feigning a sore throwing arm. He hurried home, cleaned up and got to Greater St. Paul's just as the Wednesday night prayer meeting was starting.

After the service, while leaving through the narthex, he said to the preacher, "Reverend Bob, I wonder if I could talk with you for a bit after all the other folks leaves."

"Why sure, Bud. Come on over to the Parsonage," Reverend Bob replied.

"If it's all the same to you, sir, I'd rather talk to you here in your study in private."

The preacher looked at Bud quizzically. A grin erupted on his face. With a twinkle in his eye, Reverend Bob said sure he could.

When they were finally alone Bud stammered and stalled and tried to make small talk. Finally, Reverend Bob said, "Bud, I found out a long time ago that if I had something to say that was hard to say, the best thing to do was to just spit it out. Come on, son. Say what you've got to say."

"All right, sir, I'll do it. I love your daughter. She don't know it, but I do. I'm askin' for your permission an' your blessin' to ask her to marry me."

"Don't you kid yourself, son. She knows it. She knows it as sure as she knows God made the Heaven and the earth. She's just being coy. Truth be known, she's about ready to die if you don't ask her.

"You've got my permission, and you've got my blessing. Even though you're a baseball player, you're a good man, Bud Parrott. I'd be proud to have you for a son-in-law."

That very night Bud went home with the pastor and asked Queen Esther to sit on the porch swing with him. For a while they just sat, the swing creaking as they looked at the stars.

Bud finally said, "Queenie, I been thinkin' about somethin' for a long time. I ain't … I don't have much. Not much more than the shirt on my back an' a little over three hundred dollars I got saved up. But I'm makin' good money playin' ball, an' I got the offer of a good job at the steel mill in the wintertime. I got prospects …"

"Bud Parrott," Queen Esther interrupted, "I believe that sometime between now an' mornin' you're plannin' on askin' me to marry you. Am I right or am I wrong?"

Bud smiled and looked her in the eye and, with a heart full of love, said, "Queen Esther Robinette, I love you more than I love life. I never thought I could feel this way. Will you marry me an' be my wife?"

"Bud Parrott, I thought you'd never ask. Of course, I will marry you 'cause I love you, too."

They embraced for the longest and then noticed old Rosalee looking out the parlor window, grinning and clapping her hands.

The wedding was in early October at the end of the baseball season. Of course, it was at the Greater St. Paul AME Church and was officiated by the father of the bride. Satchel Paige and all of the Crawfords were there. Even Josh Gibson, who had signed on to catch for the Crawfords the next season, was there.

The ballplayers all wanted to celebrate in their usual raucous way, a wish that could not be realized in the location of the reception — the church parlor.

After the reception, the newlyweds retired to the small house they had rented down the block from the Parsonage. Bud's teammates put on a chivaree until well after midnight, by which time the neighbors had all they wanted of it and called the police.

In the weeks that followed the young couple set up housekeeping, and Bud began his winter job in the melting room at the nearby steel mill.

His job was difficult, and it was hot. In the melting room iron ore, a very soft metal, was brought in on conveyor belts and dumped into open-ladle furnaces. The ore was melted down in furnaces and became molten semi-liquid with a temperature of thirty five hundred degrees Fahrenheit.

Next, the open-ladle furnace was tipped over, pouring the molten metal that was now steel into another ladle that was carried to the casting room by crane, where it was cast into long billets.

The red-hot billets were then conveyed into the cutting room where they were cut into workable lengths by cutting torches. Next came the cooling room where the billets were hung on large chains and swung back and forth, by hand, under running water. Once cooled the billets were stacked, loaded and shipped to large mills to be made into various steel products.

Bud's job in the melting room was very hot and dangerous. But the pay was good; and with the Depression, Bud felt fortunate to have it.

Soon Queenie became pregnant, much to Bud's delight. The baby was expected in late August or early September. Bud's biggest fear was that he would be out of town playing ball when the time came.

Spring training came and went. The regular season was in full swing. With the addition of catcher Josh Gibson, called the black Babe Ruth, the Crawfords were a genuine contender.

The regular season was right on schedule and so was Queenie. She seemed much farther along than calculated. In late July her doctor said she was carrying twins. Bed rest was ordered in August. Bud asked for and was granted permission to miss all the remaining road games.

The plan had been for Queenie to deliver at home with a midwife attending, but the twin pregnancy changed that. When labor began the last week in August, Bud and her family took her to a hospital where she was attended by a physician.

After what seemed an eternity, the physician approached the family in the waiting room and said, "Everything went fine. Mother is fine, and you have fine twin boys a little over six pounds each."

"Thank God," said Bud.

Rosalee began to weep and was comforted by Reverend Bob.

"I must tell you," said the doctor, "that the delivery was very difficult and caused considerable damage, all of which has been repaired. There can be no more pregnancies, though."

"That's okay, Doctor," said Bud. "Everthing's okay just so long as Queenie an' the babies is fine."

"Well they are fine. And they are identical."

They wanted the babies to have biblical names, so they named them Peter and Paul.

🌿 🌿 🌿 🌿

The years passed, and Bud and the Crawfords did well. Players came and went, but the nucleus of the team stayed intact.

Peter and Paul thrived. They were bright little boys: cute, intelligent and well behaved. Bud adored them, and he was more in love with Queenie than ever.

By 1935, the boys were almost three as the baseball season neared its end. The Crawfords had won both halves of the season, and the Negro World Series was to begin shortly after the twin's third birthday.

A big party was held for Peter and Paul in the church parlor on their birthday. All of Bud's teammates were there.

During the party, Oscar Charleston approached Bud and said, "Pattie, you might watch yourself. I been hearin' some of the mob is gonna bet big against the Crawfords in the World Series. One guy done come to me an' said they might need me to help 'em out. I just acted dumb 'cause I didn't know what to do."

"They ain't gonna mess with you or me, Oscar. They'll go for the big guys like Satch or Cool Papa or Josh."

"Naw they won't neither. Them guys is too big for 'em. They wants things quiet. They'll go for the little guys, so you better watch yourself."

By the middle of September it was decided that the Crawfords would play the New York Cubans in the seven-game series with three games in New York and four games in Pittsburgh.

Walking home from practice a week before the series was to begin, Bud was stopped by three men in an alleyway. One was black, large and burly. The other two were white, small and in need of shaves and showers.

The older of the two white men did all the talking. "Parrott," he said, "friends of ours got a whole lot of money bet on the Cubans. They don't care how long the series goes, they just want the Cubans to win. They want me to tell you they expect you to see that the Cubans wins."

"How you 'spect me to do that? I'm just one man."

"You can let a ball go through your legs at the right time or strike out at the right time or make a bad throw at the right time. But you do what you gotta do or you'll be sorry later. You do as you're told, an' you'll get a hundred dollars later. You mess with us, an' you'll get two broke arms." With that the men walked off.

Bud was scared; he didn't know what to do. He decided to tell no one, and maybe things would just fall into place, and he wouldn't have to throw the game.

As the series started Bud was nervous and jittery, and his performance showed it. But after awhile he settled down and played well.

After the first six games, the series was tied at three games apiece. The final game would be played in Pittsburgh. As Bud took the field at the start of the game, he noticed the burly black gangster standing behind the Crawford's dugout. When the brute had Bud's attention, he pointed a finger at Bud and walked away.

The Cubans scored two runs in the first, and the Crawfords answered with one run in the bottom of the second. The score remained two to one in favor of the Cubans going into the bottom of the ninth.

Cool Papa Bell opened the ninth with a walk and Judy Johnson singled, moving Cool Papa to third. Then Judy stole second, bringing Bud to bat with men on second and third and no outs. Bud prayed for a walk. He worked the count to three and two.

The payoff pitch was right down the middle and Bud couldn't resist it. He singled sharply to right scoring both runs, winning the game and the series.

Bud was treated as a hero, but remembering the threat, he stayed with a crowd and avoided being alone. Nothing happened. Two weeks later Bud was back in the steel mill. Just before quitting time, he reached behind him for a lever and felt a sharp blow to his right arm. The pain was severe. His wrist hung at an odd angle from his forearm.

An ambulance took Bud to the Pittsburgh Catholic Hospital where his broken arm was set and placed in a cast. The hospital kept Bud for five hours while the anesthetic wore off. As he regained consciousness, Bud became impatient to get home to his family.

Bud alternately ran and walked the twenty-one blocks from the hospital to his house. The exertion seemed to make his head groggier, and he was in too much pain to run for more than two or three blocks at a time.

When he got within a few blocks of home, he noticed black smoke billowing in the vicinity of his house. He began to run as fast as he could, and when he was within a block of his home he was grabbed and embraced by his father-in-law.

Tears were streaming down the large black man's face as he said, "It's your house, Bud. They're gone. Queen Esther and the boys were in the house. They are all gone. And Rosalee is gone too."

Bud collapsed in tears and cried out. "No! My God, no! Queenie, Peter, Paul … It's all my fault. Oh, my God! I killed my family."

"No you didn't, son," said Reverend Bob through his tears. "I had a feeling the gamblers tried to bribe you. Queenie wouldn't have wanted you to be dishonest. You didn't do this. Bad people did."

"What will I do now? Oh, my God! What am I to do?" cried Bud.

"You'll do what colored folks have had to do ever since they were brought to this country. You'll persevere. That's all we can do, son. We gotta just pull ourselves up by our bootstraps, trust in God and keep on living … doing the best we can."

The funeral was almost more than Bud could bear; and were it not for the strength and the faith in God of his father-in-law, he couldn't have gotten through it. Reverend Bob preached the service with tears streaming down his face. Bud's Crawford teammates were the only people left to sit in the family section with him. Even Gus Greenlee and Woogie were there. Every foot of every pew was occupied.

After the opening remarks and prayers, the choir sang "Rock of Ages," "Nearer My God to Thee" and finally "Amazing Grace." Then Reverend Robinette stood up in the pulpit and, in a deep and resonant voice, began the eulogy.

"I stand before you today," he began, "to say goodbye for awhile to four wonderful people. One was old and had lived most of her earthly life. She was the mother of my wife and had to stand by in her middle years and watch her daughter laid to rest. Her name was Rosalee Jones, and she was a good, kind, God-fearing woman.

"One was young and just starting out in life — a wife and a mother. She was beautiful and kind and also God-fearing. Her name was Queen Esther Robinette Parrott, and she was my daughter and Rosalee's granddaughter. She was the wife of Bud Parrott, a kind and gentle man.

"And then there are Queenie's two little boys, Peter Parrott and Paul Parrott, twins barely three years old. They hadn't even begun to live in this world hardly at all, and now they've gone to live in the next with their mama and their great-grandmama. They have gone to meet Jesus, face to face. Along with Him, they'll get to meet my wife, their grandmama, and all their other kin. They've gone to a far better place than where they've been.

"So in one instant four earthly lives have ended, and four heavenly lives have begun. All Bud and I have left is each other and our friends. Both our families have left us, and we grieve for them, because we miss them, and we love them.

"These loved ones of ours lost their lives because this good man, out there crying among you, could do no wrong. Doing right cost him his family and a broken arm to boot. He's feeling guilty because he did right, and he's wishing he had done wrong so those bad men wouldn't have killed his family.

"His doing right cost me all the family I have and all the family I'm ever gonna have. But I'm here to tell you I'm proud of this man, and I know my daughter in Heaven is proud of him, too. Jesus taught us to do right, and we'll be rewarded, and Bud Parrott will be rewarded, for some day he will be in Paradise forever with those he loves.

"The Bible says, 'I know that my redeemer liveth, and that he shall stand at the latter day upon the earth. And though this body be destroyed, yet shall I see God, whom I shall see for myself, and mine eyes shall behold, and not as a stranger.'

"So we say so long for now sweet children of God. We'll see you again in the sweet by and by." And then he wept.

In the days that followed, Bud was inconsolable. He was persuaded by his father-in-law to move into the Parsonage with him, at least for the time being. He could not work due to his arm, and he knew he never wanted to play baseball again. At first his teammates came to call, but before long their visits stopped.

Bud was at a loss as to how to spend his time. Most days he just started out walking and ended up wherever his feet took him. In time, the acute pain ended and was replaced by an ache and an emptiness that he knew would remain forever.

By December his arm was well enough for the cast to be removed, but he had lost most of the mobility he previously had in the wrist. He could never play ball again. His bum wrist would prevent it, even if he wanted to play; and he certainly didn't want to.

As the winter snows came, Bud found himself walking farther and longer. The cold was miserable; it magnified his discomfort. He felt the cold and let it punish him.

One day he walked far past the edge of the city and wandered down snow-covered rural roads. Bud stopped on a path at the edge of a dark wood. There he built a small fire, sat and contemplated the flames and smoke.

As twilight surrounded him, Bud spoke into the darkness. "Queenie, I miss you somethin' awful. I miss my little boys, too. Y'all was the only family I'll ever have. Missin' an' hurtin' and cryin' ain't gonna help at all, though. So I gotta put that behind me an' do as your daddy said. I gotta pull myself together an' keep on a-livin'.

"I just cain't do it here. I gotta leave this place an' never come back. I hate it I won't be able to come to your graves no more, but I'll have all of you in my heart. Wherever I go an' whatever I do, you'll all be there with me.

"I know what I gotta do now. I gotta go home, back to the South, back to Jackson County, back to the farmland. That's where I belong. I thought I belonged here, but I don't. Ever since they taken y'all from me, I don't belonged here.

"I ain't got no money, 'cause it burned up in the fire, but I'll get there even if'n I have to ride the rails again.

"I promise you one thing. There ain't never gonna be another woman for me, 'cause I've had the best an' nary a one could measure up to you."

As he walked back into the city, the moon and stars finally shone through the clouds. The air was cold enough to sting the insides of his nostrils. Bud looked up at the stars as he walked. Finally, he was at peace.

Having decided to leave, Bud only had to pick the time of his leaving. He chose not to leave until after Christmas, reasoning that the holidays would be a bad time for Reverend Bob. Bud didn't want the Reverend to go through the holiday season alone.

Bud knew he would have to make some money to get home on, and he would have to make it fast. With his wrist still sore and stiff, manual labor was not an option. Bud went to Gus Greenlee.

Gus was in his office above the Crawford Bar and Grill.

"Come on in, Pattie," Gus said when he saw Bud approaching. "Have a seat. I been worried about you. Hadn't seen you since the funeral. Glad to see you up an' about. Man, I'm sorry about what happened to your wife an' kids."

"Thanks, Gus. I come to tell you I ain't gonna be playin' no more ball. My wrist is ruined, an' I ain't got the heart for it no way."

"Damn, I hate that, Pattie. You're the best second baseman in the league. Satch headed for greener pastures, an' I hear some of the other players is leavin', so I'll likely not have much of a team next year. Reckon there's any way I can get you to change your mind?"

"Naw; my mind's made up. You might as well stop callin' me Pattie. I ain't a ballplayer no more.

"Naw," Bud continued, "I'm goin' home, back to Arkansas an' the farm. I ain't heard from my mama in near 'bout five years. I'm gonna go see her an' then see if Mr. Hugh Monte McGillicuddy will give me my old job back."

"I don't blame you, Bud," said Gus. "Pittsburgh ain't been too kind to you, has it? It took guts for you to stand up to them gamblers, an' I'm proud of you for doin' it. But them guys ain't over their mad yet. I don't blame you for gettin' out."

"I ain't scared of them, Gus. I wish I could run into 'em. I swear I'd kill 'em on sight."

"Them boys is mean to the core, Bud. You see them; you given 'em a wide berth. You ain't no match for them; you take my word for it."

"Well, that ain't why I'm here, Gus. I cain't leave 'fore Christmas, 'cause I don't wanta leave Reverend Bob to have to spend Christmas alone. I figure on leavin' on New Year's Eve an' start 1936 with Pittsburgh behind me.

"I need to make some money fast, an' I cain't do no real work yet with my messed up arm. I wanta run the numbers for you between now an' New Year's. I'll take for pay whatever you say is fair."

"I cain't let you do that," replied Gus. "If them gamblers was to see you, they'd kill you for sure. I cain't let that happen.

"I'll tell you what, though. By winnin' that series for me you made me a bunch of money, an' I had a wad ridin' on it, too. I figure I owe you somethin' extra. I'm gonna give you a bonus." Gus pulled three one hundred dollar bills out of his pocket and held them out to Bud.

"I cain't take your charity nor your pity," said Bud. "I aim to work for what you give me an' rightly earn it."

"You earned it, Bud. By God, you sure earned it! Now take this money."

Bud was silent for a moment and felt as if he were about to cry. Then he composed himself and said, "Three hunnerd's too much, but I'll take a hunnerd. That'll get me home. Soon as I can I'll wire it back to you."

"Naw, Bud, take the hunnerd an' you keep it. I'll consider it an insult if you send it back to me."

"Thanks, Gus. You're a good man, an' I appreciate all you done for me."

"It's me oughta be thankin' you. You got more guts than any three players I ever seen. Everybody else on that team woulda throwed that game," said Gus.

Bud walked out of the Crawford Bar and Grill for the last time, tears streaming down his cheeks.

Christmas was bleak at the Parsonage. Neither man could bring himself to put up a tree. Reverend Bob had services on Christmas Eve and Christmas morning. Miss Mozelle Barton, a retired school teacher and the oldest member of the church, invited Bud and the Reverend to Christmas dinner, and they gladly accepted.

They walked home after the meal in a heavy snowfall, the sky darker than usual for midafternoon in early winter. Walking with faces shielded by scarves from the driving snow, their silence was broken when Bud said, "Bob, I'm gonna be leavin' before long. I'm goin' home, back to the farm in Arkansas, back to my roots."

"I know, son, I know. I've just been wonderin' how long it would take you to make up your mind to do it. I hate for you to go, but I don't blame you. There's nothin' here for you now except hurt and pain.

"You'll need money. I don't have much, but I can spare you twenty."

"Gus Greenlee fixed me up with plenty money to do me. An' the church folks fixed me up with plenty clothes. I wonder if you got a grip I can use to pack my stuff in."

"Sure I do, son. You're welcome to it. I wish you didn't have to go, but I understand. You're the only family I got now, an' I'm gonna miss you."

So all the bridges were crossed, and now all that remained was waiting for New Year's Eve. Bud felt foolish for waiting. Maybe he should pack and leave. But somehow, it was important for him to begin his trip and his new life with the New Year.

On December 31, with another driving snowstorm outside, Bud began to pack. He had a suit, tie and dress shirt, two extra work shirts, a heavy sweater and an extra pair of pants. In addition to the brogans he wore, he had a pair of dress shoes and his work boots from the foundry. He decided to wear a heavy Mackinaw jacket, a knit watch cap and woolen gloves for the trip.

The last thing he packed was a two-foot square pasteboard box wrapped in cellophane. Inside it were the chronicles of Sunshine Sam. Luckily, Bud had loaned them to Reverend Bob for his pleasure and enlightenment; at the Reverend's house they had escaped the fire. Except for baseball paraphernalia, they were Bud's remaining treasure.

Bud and his father-in-law took their noon meal together in silence. When it ended, Bud rose and went into his room.

A few moments later, Bud reappeared in the dining room wearing his coat, cap and gloves and carrying the suitcase Bob had given him. Reverend Bob rose and escorted Bud to the front door. On the porch they shook hands and then embraced.

Bud looked into Reverend Bob's eyes, thinking how old and sad he looked. Then each man smiled, the Reverend nodded, and without a word, Bud turned away and walked into the snow.

As he walked to the train depot, Bud realized he was closing a door forever to a part of his life — a wonderful, brief part that now was finished.

Night was falling as he arrived at the station. Bright lights shone through the depot's tall windows, promising warmth and comfort. Bud found an open ticket window and told the agent he was going to Newport in Northeast Arkansas. He was sold a one-way ticket to Memphis through Columbus, Ohio, with an overnight layover in Cincinnati. From there he would travel through Louisville, Kentucky, to Nashville, Tennessee, where he would spend another night. On the third day, he would arrive in Memphis, on the Mississippi River. How he would travel the last eighty miles to Newport was a problem he would not be able to solve until arriving in Memphis.

After buying his ticket, Bud bought a ham sandwich and coffee. He took a seat by a large pot-bellied, coal-burning stove. He noticed the few people in the waiting room were mostly white, with only him and two other blacks present. Soon he would be back in the part of the country that did not allow the races to mix, and he sensed a foreboding. Still he would be home, where — when the races did mingle — it was likely to be with laughter and cheer.

What would his mother be like after sixteen years' absence? Bud longed to be with her again. If she had dictated any letters to him during the past five years, the postal system had not been able to deliver them. Bud realized his heart raced as he worried about the silence.

Bud remembered Utah Brown, Mr. Hugh Monte, and Sixty, the man Mr. Hugh Monte had found as a baby. He had been abandoned by the side of Highway 69 near Jacksonport, Arkansas. The only name the foundling ever had was Sixty Nine, and he was called Sixty for short. He knew Sixty, who was a real character, would cheer him up.

The warmth of the fire lulled Bud to sleep. Shortly after ten o'clock he was awakened by the ticket agent's call to board the train.

The car in which Bud was seated had only six passengers. This pleased him, because the last thing he wanted was conversation.

Bud had nearly fallen back to sleep by the time the train pulled out of the station. City buildings soon became sparse and slowly the train gathered speed. By the time the conductor came through and announced it was midnight and now 1936, Bud could no longer see the lights of Pittsburgh. Glad to have Pittsburgh behind him, he was yet sad knowing that Queenie, Peter and Paul would rest there forever, never to be visited by husband and father again.

Bud had been raised by a mother and a grandmother. After his grandmother died and his mother married the blacksmith, he had been alone except for the four years he had Queenie and the three years he had Peter and Paul. They had been a real family, and he knew he would never be part of a family again.

Bud knew his father-in-law was right when he said colored folks just had to trust in God and keep on living, doing the best they could. That is what he would do. He would do it where he knew he belonged, where he was confident of his standing. He would do it in the South, his home.

The rail car was cold, the night dark; and a heavy snow was falling. Even in his Mackinaw, Bud was chilled to the bone. Gathering his things, he moved to the far end of the car, near a small coal-burning stove. By reversing the seat in front of him so that the two double seats faced each other, he could lean back in one and use the other as a footrest.

Bud pulled his cap down over his ears and turned up the collar of his Mackinaw. The clickety-clack of the wheels and the warmth of the fire had just about lulled him to sleep when a thin, gray-headed black man with sunken eyes and a hacking cough approached him.

"How 'bout sharin' the fire with me, friend? You're takin' up four seats the way you're sittin'," he said.

Bud said nothing but scooted over, offering the man a seat. The man sat opposite Bud and put his feet up in the seat next to Bud. His clothes were worn, his shoes patched, and his breath smelled of liquor.

"I'm Roscoe Peabody of the Memphis Peabodys, an' I'm a-goin home to see my mama. What's your name, boy?"

"Bud Parrott."

"Well, I'll be! Named after a bird, is you? All us Peabodys in Memphis, we likes birds. We even got some ducks in our hotel. Them ducks parade to the pool ever' morning. How 'bout you, Parrott? You spend your days swimming?"

Bud just looked away and tried to ignore the man.

"Come on, boy. It's gonna be a long trip. Why don't you be sociable now. Here, have a drink." He held a half-empty pint of whiskey out toward Bud.

"No thanks, I ain't a drinker," replied Bud.

"Parrott, you near 'bout the saddest lookin' black I ever seen. Come on, a little liquor'll cheer you up. A lot of liquor will wipe your cares away. Come on, now, you need a little cheerin' up."

Bud finally took the bottle, turned it up and took two large swallows. The liquor burned his throat. He coughed.

"Quick. Take another swig to stop the cough," Roscoe said, handing the bottle back to Bud.

For thirty minutes the bottle passed back and forth until it was empty. By then Bud was feeling light-headed and warm inside. Everything Roscoe said seemed funny to Bud, and soon his tongue was as loose as Roscoe's.

"You ain't really kin to no hotel people, Roscoe. Now is you?"

"Why, hell no. They wouldn't even let me in the back door of that hotel. I ain't never knowed who my daddy was, so I figured I could pick me out any name I wanted. I decided a long time ago I'd just be a Peabody, by God!"

"Same way with me, 'cept my old granny was who give me my name. She said my daddy was a fast-talker who flew away like a bird, so she named me for a talkin' bird."

They rambled on into the night. For the first time in weeks Bud could laugh. His mind wasn't filled with death, loss and guilt. Roscoe even taught Bud how to roll his own cigarette, and by morning the two of them had smoked a whole can of Prince Albert.

With morning came a headache and a raspy throat for Bud, but Roscoe was fast asleep. He awoke when the train pulled into Columbus.

"Well, this here's where I get off," said Roscoe.

"I thought you was goin' to Memphis," replied Bud.

"Hell, naw. I ain't lost nothin' in Memphis. You better get off with me. You don't need none of that Southern hospitality they dishes out for colored boys neither."

"Naw, I'm headed for Arkansas an' back to the farm where I belong," said Bud. "See you again someday."

"Bye, then. But here. Take this here half-pint to keep you warm an' here's some more Prince Albert, too."

Bud thanked him, took the liquor and tobacco and settled back for a long, lonesome trip.

Between Columbus and Cincinnati Bud became quite adept at rolling his own cigarettes. He found he liked tobacco, and was surprised that he had never tried it before. He respected, maybe even feared liquor, however. The bottle Roscoe had left him went untouched.

Except for one stop when all male passengers had to get out and shovel snow off the tracks, the trip was uneventful. Shoveling snow alongside the conductor was welcome exercise. It warmed him and improved his mood.

After a night of sleeping on a bench in the Cincinnati depot, Bud freshened himself in the men's room and then had breakfast in the cafe. It was his first meal in thirty hours.

By noon, he was on another train headed to Louisville, where he transferred to Nashville. He arrived in Nashville after midnight and catnapped the rest of the night in the depot. During the night, he treated himself to a small taste of Roscoe's liquor.

After breakfast in the railroad cafe, Bud bought two cans of Bull Durham tobacco and four packs of cigarette paper.

Memphis was only a hundred and ninety miles, but the train stopped at every little depot along the way, so the trip took most of the day.

At the Memphis depot, Bud learned that there was no rail connection to Northeast Arkansas. The only way to get there by rail was to go west to Little Rock on the Cotton Belt and then north to Newport on the Missouri-Pacific. Anxious as he was by now to get home, Bud decided to try his luck at hitchhiking.

There was a chill in to the air that made walking uncomfortable. Bud hoped he would catch a ride east of the Mississippi. That was not to be, however; and he arrived at the Mississippi River bridge afoot.

The bridge was so similar to the one Bud had crossed in Vicksburg so many years ago. Here, too, rail traffic was in the center of the bridge. On either side was automobile traffic — one way was going east on the south side of the tracks, and one way was going west on the north side. Outermost on either side of the bridge was a narrow footpath with waist-high rails.

Bud began the mile long walk across the bridge as twilight settled. Darkness was not far off. The stiff wind was bone-chilling cold. Walking into the wind, Bud couldn't help but reflect on the time between his two crossings. He had become a steel worker and a professional ballplayer, a husband, father and then a widower. Now his destiny was to be alone, always alone. He felt Queenie's presence, and for a moment, he considered jumping into the dark water below. But to do so would be a sin, an insult to the memory of Queenie. He also feared that suicide wouldn't get him into Heaven; that thought alone was enough to make him stop. If there was a Heaven, and Reverend Bob had assured him there was, then he most certainly wanted to get there and be with Queenie again.

So he walked the long walk, high above the big river. As the full moon rose, he entered Arkansas on the west bank of the river. Cold and windburned, he was home at last.

❧ ❧ ❧ ❧

Bud walked into West Memphis and found the colored section of town. At a cafe whose windows were filled with buzzing neon lights, Bud warmed himself with coffee and a plate of pancakes. An elderly black man offered him a ride the forty-five miles into Forrest City.

It was nearing midnight when the old man let Bud out under the only traffic light Bud had seen since leaving West Memphis. Bud pointed himself north and began walking through Forrest City along the Jonesboro highway. Within an hour he was picked up by a trucker who let him ride in the back of his truck to Jonesboro.

Another ride soon got him to Waldenburg before sunup. There Bud knew he was within thirty miles of home.

The gravel road from Waldenburg to Newport was frozen solid and abandoned in the middle of the night. Bud knew he had a long, cold walk ahead of him. Three hours later he walked into the tiny village of Amagon, and by the time he arrived there the dawn was breaking at his back.

The sun was up when he crossed the Cache River bridge, and shortly thereafter he was given a ride by a farmer in an old Model A pickup truck. The farmer was headed home from duck hunting in the Cache River bottoms. He let Bud out at the Village Creek bridge, and Bud knew he was three miles from home.

The brisk walking — and the sun at his back — warmed him. As Bud topped the levee at the edge of Newport, he stopped and took it all in. The town had changed very little. Barren trees whistled in the midwinter light. He knew very little went on at this time of the year, farmers rested and reminisced. The spring planting season would be upon them soon enough.

As Bud looked over the town, he realized he loved the place. He wished Queenie could be right there beside him, seeing it with him. But he knew that as he said hello to this childhood home of his, he must also say goodbye to Queenie. She was the center of his life in Pittsburgh, but did not belong to this part. So here he was — home. He had left it in the dark of a hot summer night. He returned in the light of a cold winter day. All that was left for him to do now was to find his mother and then look up Mr. Hugh Monte and get his old job back.

The levee he stood on encircled the town and kept White River floods from inundating the place. Only once in Bud's memory had the river topped the levee, and that was long ago. About two-thirds up the inside of the levee was a six-foot wide terrace on which the Rock Island Railroad tracks had been in earlier times. The tracks were long gone; grass covered the old rail bed.

Bud walked the abandoned rail bed, sensing his approach to the colored section of town, where it met the levee. Soon he could see his old neighborhood. The old shack he had grown up in was gone. No smoke rose from the chimney of the house his mother and her blacksmith had shared.

When he opened the unpainted door, Bud found the house was long abandoned. Not a stick of his mother's furniture remained. The full force of his sixteen-year absence fell on Bud's shoulders. Then he remembered that Utah Brown lived somewhere near the colored school, so he headed in that direction.

An old man pushing a steaming hot tamale cart pointed out Utah's house. Bud bought two tamales from him and ate as he walked. He had forgotten how delicious James' hot tamales were. Rumor was that James made his tamales from the meat of stray cats, but Bud had never believed it.

The door was opened by Odessa Brown, Utah's wife. "Miz Brown, you don't remember me, but I'm Bud Parrott. Is Utah to home?" asked Bud.

"Why, Bud Parrott, 'course I 'member you. You Miss Julia's boy. Lawdee! You been gone a long time. You done growed plumb up."

"Yes'm. Is Utah home? I really needs to see him."

"Hey, Utah! Come look what the cats drug up," she yelled. Utah came to the door as Odessa was inviting Bud in. Bud knew him to be about ten years older than himself, and he was shocked to see how really old he looked. He held out his hand, and Utah took it.

"Bud Parrott! Boy, I thought you done gone an' left here for good. What you doin' back here?"

They sat down in ladder-back chairs facing a Franklin stove and leaned forward to warm their hands as they talked.

"It's a long story, Utah. Too long to go into now. I come back 'cause this here is my home. This is where I belongs. I'm lookin' for my mama. You know where she's stayin' now?"

"Boy, you don't know? Why, you mama caught the cancer four or five years ago an' didn't last a month. Nobody wrote an' told you?" asked Utah.

Bud sat in silence for awhile, his eyes darting first to the floor and then the stove. Finally he said, "Mama couldn't write nor read. I wrote her letters an' sent 'em to Mother Parks to read to her. I never heard nothin' back in the last five or six years."

"Mother Parks died in thirty or thirty-one, I ain't sure which. That idiot child of her'n, old Ezra, he burned up all her stuff an' near

106

'bout burned down her house. They taken him away an' put him somewheres. I never knowed where," said Utah. "What you gonna do now, Bud?"

"I guess I'll find me a place to stay an' go see Mr. Hugh Monte about gettin' me a job."

"Mr. Hugh Monte sold that farm of his'n here while back an' taken Sixty an' moved somewhere's down in the Delta Country on a great big farm he bought. They say he got eight or ten thousand acres an' more mules than you can count. He wanted me to go with him, but I got this here young wife an' several churrens. I thanked him but stayed put.

"I'm workin' for the new owner of Mr. Hugh Monte's farm, old Henry Wood. He's a tough old fart an' don't take nothin' off of nobody, but he's fair. His boy, the one they call Big Ike, he does most of the bossin', though. He's a real good man an' fair, too; but don't mess with him none at night 'cause he gets to drinkin' after dark, an' gets meaner'n a snake when he's drunk.

"You go talk to Mr. Henry, or better yet Big Ike. You'll get you a job. They lives at Tuckerman, so you'll have to go see 'em there."

Bud thanked him and politely declined Odessa's invitation to stay for the noon meal. He walked out into the dirt street and for a while just walked aimlessly. Now he was really alone; no living soul he could claim as kin.

Tuckerman was ten miles north, so Bud decided to wait until the next day to make the trip. He decided to find a room, at least temporarily. He wandered around until he came to a two-story frame building with a sign over the door that said "Madame Lena's Boarding House … Palms Read and Fortunes Told."

Bud knocked on the door and was greeted by an enormously obese black woman of about sixty. Her head was covered with a red bandana, and her dress was as big as a tent.

"What can I do for you, boy. I'm Madame Lena. You want your fortune told? It'll cost you a nickel."

"No ma'am. I needs a room. I don't know how long I'll be needin' it. Depends on where I find work."

"Come on in. I got three or four rooms left, all of 'em upstairs. Go on up. I don't like climbin' them stairs. Pick out whichever one you want an' store your things. It'll cost you two dollars a week, an' for that you also get breakfast an' supper.

"There ain't no dinner served here, 'cause I expect all my roomers to be out workin' durin' the daytime. Cain't have no womens in here neither. You hear me, boy?"

"Yes'm. You don't need to worry about me an' no women though," Bud replied.

"You ain't no queer, is you? Now I sure don't allow no queers around here. You ain't, is you?"

"Oh, no ma'am. It's just I ain't too long ago lost my wife, an' I ain't got over it yet."

"What she do, run off with another man?"

"No ma'am. She died."

"Oh. I'm sorry for you then. What you say your name was?"

"Bud Parrott."

"Well, get settled, Bud. There's a slop jar under ever bed, an' the privy's out back. The washin' pump's on the back porch. Supper's at seven sharp. You miss it, an' you go hungry 'til mornin'."

❧ ❧ ❧ ❧

Bud spent a fitful night trying to sleep that first night at Madame Lena's. He wondered if coming back to Newport had been the right thing for him to do. His mother, Sixty and Mr. Hugh Monte all were gone. The only person left from the old days was Utah, unless, maybe Hillard and his brother, Junior, were still at the farm. He knew he had friends in Pittsburgh and even in Birmingham, but he had almost no one here and certainly no family. Never in his life had he felt more alone.

Morning finally came, and a good warm breakfast improved his spirits. After breakfast, he began walking toward Tuckerman and, hopefully, a job.

He walked through East Newport and then north on Highway 67 until he came to the viaduct crossing the Missouri-Pacific Railroad tracks. There a three-man work crew was just finishing a job. As they were loading their tools onto their speeder, Bud approached them.

"Y'all wouldn't be headed north, would you?" he asked.

"Yeah," said the largest of the three black men. "You need a ride?"

"Sure do," replied Bud. "I'm goin' to Tuckerman."

"Well, hop on then; but we gotta let you off 'fore we get into town. Cain't let the boss man see you a-ridin.'"

So Bud rode the rest of the way into Tuckerman on the speeder, got off at the edge of town, thanked the men for the ride and walked into town. He asked for, and received, directions to Henry Wood's house on the highway in the middle of town.

When he arrived at Henry Wood's house, he went around to the back and knocked on the kitchen door. The maid answered his knock and told Bud that no one was home and referred him to Isaac Henry's house.

❧ ❧ ❧ ❧

Here is where Bud Parrot's story intersected my own. At Isaac Henry Wood's house, Bud went to the rear of the house, as was his habit, and knocked at the back door. Naomi, Ike's wife and my mother, answered.

"Mornin', Ma'am," said Bud. "I'd like to see Mr. Isaac Henry if he be home. I'm lookin' for farm work."

My father, overhearing the conversation, went to the door and introduced himself. "I'm Big Ike," he said. "You don't have to 'mister' me. An' if you come to my house to see me, you come to the front door like a man. Don't come lookin' for me with your hat in your hand. Look me in the face, eye to eye, man to man."

Bud smiled and said, "To look you eye to eye I'd have to stand on a stool, as big as you is."

That brought a hearty laugh from Big Ike and endeared Bud to him from that time on.

"Come on into the kitchen." said Ike. "What's your name, anyway?"

"Bud Parrott, Mr. Ike."

"Dammit, don't you be 'misterin'' me now. 'Mister' my old man. I mean it now; you call me Big Ike. Have a seat there at the table. What can I do for you?"

"I needs work. I just come back home from up North. I used to work the fields for Mr. Hugh Monte, but I heard he done sold out to you an' your daddy. So I come here to ask you for work."

"We'll see about that," said Big Ike. "What did you do up North, anyways."

"I took off from here when I was just a kid, about seventeen, I reckon. I left Newport thinkin' I'd go off an' make me some money an' be somebody, but it didn't turn out that way, an' I come back home where I belong."

"But what kinda work you been doin'?"

"First I went to Birminham, Alabama, an' worked in a pipe factory. Then to Pittsburgh where I was a ballplayer an' worked in the steel mill there."

"Were you a professional ballplayer? In the colored league?"

"Yessir," replied Bud. "I played for the Birminham Black Barons an' then the Pittsburgh Crawfords."

"Well, why in hell did you quit an' come back here?" asked Big Ike.

"Got my arm broke in a accident at the mill an' couldn't pitch or bat no more, so I had to quit. I didn't like it up North no ways; so I just come on home. Now I'm near 'bout broke an' I sure do need a job."

"If you worked in a steel mill you know what hard work is. You any good with tools? Can you fix things?"

"I sure can," answered Bud.

"Where you stayin'?"

"At Madame Lena's in Newport."

"Tell you what. I'm gonna give you a job, but you're no field hand. I'm gonna make you my right-hand man at the old McGillicuddy farm out from Newport. I got a little cabin there you can live in. Folks been stealin' me blind with nobody stayin' on the place.

"Your job'll be to watch out, and make sure nobody steals from me. You can keep up the place an' keep all the tools an' equipment in good shape. There's a tractor you can use for plowin'. You can be the boss man for my field hands.

"I'll do right by you, but you better not turn on me or do wrong by me, 'cause if you do I'll have your balls in a sack."

"I'll do right by you Mr. ... Big Ike. I'll be honest, an' I'll be square. You can count on me," said Bud.

"That's the way I had it figured, Bud. That's why I'm offerin' you the job."

Thus began a fifteen-year association of Bud Parrott and my family.

Big Ike loaned Bud his thirty-two Ford pickup truck to drive back to Newport and get his things. He was to return to Tuckerman at first light the next morning, pick up Big Ike and go to see the Jacksonport farm. Naomi packed him a ham sandwich to eat on the way back to Newport.

"You sho' come up in the world quick to be so new in town," Madame Lena said when she heard Bud's news.

"Yes'm, I guess I have. I got me a job on Mr. Wood's farm out to Jacksonport. That there's Big Ike's truck. He's gonna move me onto the place to be his overseer an' his right-hand man. I'll be a-movin out there in the mornin' so I won't need your room after tonight. I reckon you owe me about a dollar an' a quarter since I won't be staying here no more after tonight."

"Huh uh," she said. "How you come up with that, boy?"

"'I paid you two dollars for seven days, an' I ain't gonna be stayin' but for two."

"I didn't say nothin' 'bout refundin' no money," she argued. "Boy, I wasn't gonna say nothin', but you better be careful. I done read your fortune. If'n you go back out to that old McGillicuddy farm, you'll be dead inside of two weeks. I ain't sure just how, but you gonna be crushed to death. You just better stay here where you're at an forget about that farm."

That fortune really scared Bud. He didn't believe it, but his disbelief wasn't strong enough to assuage his fear. "You ain't read my fortune. You ain't even seen my palms," retorted Bud.

"Yes I have, boy. I snuck up in your room last night while you was sleeping, an' I read your palm. I sure did. An' it ain't too good, I tell you. Now you just better do like I say an' stay where you're at an' forget about that dollar refund."

Bud knew for sure then that Madame Lena was lying, because he had slept very little. He was a very light sleeper; and anyone entering his room was sure to wake him, particularly anyone as obese as Lena. He was amused, though, for she had managed to get the refund in question down to a dollar when he had mentioned a dollar and a quarter.

"Naw, Madame Lena, I ain't worried about dyin' no way. One of them old voodoo womens down in Louisiana charmed me with a voodoo hex a long time ago. She said I'm gonna live to be ninety years old, an' anyone ever try to read my palm or tell my fortune is gonna die of syphilis of the brain."

"Now, boy, don't you story me none. I ain't gonna stand for that," she said, but Bud could tell she was taken aback.

"I ain't teasin', Miss Lena. That old woman told me I wouldn't marry 'til I was seventy, an' my last child was gonna be born when I was eighty-eight. She said never to let nobody read my palm, 'cause if I did let 'em they'd sure as the world get the syph. That's why I wouldn't let you tell my fortune yesterday.

"But I tell you what. You just gimme that dollar you mentioned, an' I'll be outa here bright an' early tomorrow, an' you won't be tempted to read my fortune no more an' get the syph."

Lena wasn't sure what to make of Bud's tale. She knew she was safe, though; because, of course, she had not read his palm.

"I tell you what, Mr. Bud Parrott. I'll give you six bits back; take it or leave it."

Okay, Miss Lena. I'll take the six bits. You may need the rest of that money to buy you some syphilis medicine," he said.

So Lena handed over seventy-five cents and went to the kitchen in a huff, and Bud went to his room to await supper.

At first light the next morning, Bud picked up Big Ike, and they drove to the farm. Bud was surprised to see how run down the place was, but said nothing.

Big Ike spoke up and said, "After Hugh Monte bought that big farm down in the Delta he just neglected this place. The only hands he left here were Utah and Hillard and that little idiot, Junior. Utah's all right, but he don't have much gumption, and Hillard ain't worth shootin'. That's why I'm puttin' you in charge, Bud. You got some sense, an' I got a feelin' I can trust you."

"You sure can, Mr. Wood; you sure can," replied Bud.

"Now, Bud, don't you 'mister' me an' don't you 'sir' me. I'm your boss, sure, but I ain't your master. You're older than me, too. I mean it, you call me Big Ike!"

Then he leaned back, grabbed his overalls with both thumbs and grinned real big. Both men burst out laughing.

The swayed-roof house Bud was to live in needed new screen in the door. Five windowpanes were broken, and some of the porch boards were broken out; but with a little paint, it would serve Bud just fine. The small sitting room had a pot-bellied stove. The bedroom was barely big enough for the bed and a set of drawers. In the kitchen stood a black wood-burning cook stove and a lead-lined icebox. The sink was built into a bench under a window and a long-handled hand pump stood over it. The one-hole privy out back looked like it needed new door hinges.

An empty dog pen filled the space between the privy and a sickly grape arbor. Past the arbor was a large barn for livestock. Bud had to explore it. Its milking stalls were empty. A hayloft ran down the center of the barn. At either end of the loft were doors; outside each door hung a block and tackle for lifting bales of hay into the loft.

The countryside was as Bud remembered it to be in the dead of winter, desolate and barren. Bud knew that, come spring, the land would prove bountiful and beautiful.

Bud moved in, and Big Ike took the truck back to town. Big Ike promised a pair of mules the next day. Mules would be Bud's transportation; he could ride a mule bareback or hitch the pair to an old wagon left in the barn.

A fifty-pound block of ice the men brought that morning would keep his milk, bacon and eggs for several days.

With an ax he found in the barn, Bud cut and split firewood the rest of the morning. By midafternoon he had fires in both of his stoves. After seeing to the outhouse door and oiling the kitchen water pump, Bud fried eggs and bacon for supper in a warm, cozy house.

After supper he sat by the fire in the living room and opened the stove door so he could see the flames. The only other light in the house was a candle on the table beside his chair.

Watching the flames dance, Bud listened to the wind beat sheaves of dry grass against the house. The fire's crackle and the whistling of the winter wind seemed like just the right amount of noise. How unlike the sounds of Pittsburgh, he thought. Remembering the sounds of the city — traffic, sirens, neighbors and mill sounds — he realized now how he had missed the silence of the country.

Too many folks, that's what he thought of the city. Folks who had forgotten — or never knew — how to be simply kind, thoughtful and neighborly. The city made people harsh; it turned their hearts ugly, their brains selfish. It brought out the evil, the meanness in men. To

Bud the city meant gamblers, numbers-runners and mobsters. All that once was exciting, energizing and wonderful about the city was now lost to him. The city was, and would forever be, the place that took Queenie and his boys away from him.

Now he had a house, a farm with a barn and two mules, and a job as boss man. Big Ike trusted him. Bud's heart felt full. He had all he could ever hope for or expect.

He fell asleep in the chair, warmed by the fire, in a house he could call his own. Queenie appeared in a dream, smiling at him, telling him she knew he was home, telling how she could now, finally, rest in peace.

At dawn, when he was awakened by the crowing of a rooster, he knew he was where he should be.

The years passed and the farm prospered. Bud came to love his work and his home. His affection for Big Ike grew. The two men became friends, although both men knew that each had his place in Southern society.

Within their first year together, Ike began to take Bud with him whenever he had to make short trips to Jonesboro, Clarendon or Wynne. Always, Big Ike drove a yellow Chevy, and Bud sat in the front seat with him. Big Ike and Bud smoked one Camel after another on those trips, and Ike told one tall tale after another.

Soon Bud was spinning tales as well. He told Ike of his baseball days, of Sunshine Sam and the hobo jungles, of the pipe company in Birmingham and the steel mill in Pittsburgh. He told him of Satch and Cool Papa and Josh, of Gus Greenlee and Woogie. Bud never told Big Ike about the way Queenie hugged him when he returned from a road game; he never told Ike about his sons, how they hugged his legs. He never even told Big Ike that he had ever been married.

On a trip to Blytheville, they started talking baseball. Bud argued that the best colored players were as good as, or better than, most white major leaguers.

"Nobody, an' I mean nobody, is as good as Babe Ruth or Ty Cobb," Big Ike said.

"Well, I ain't never seen Babe Ruth," said Bud, "but I seen Ty Cobb. We played a exhibition against the Detroit Tigers one time, an' Satchel Paige struck out Ty Cobb twice, an' old Cobb said he'd never play no coloreds again."

"The hell you say!" exclaimed Big Ike.

"No kiddin'," said Bud. "Ty Cobb waren't no better than Cool Papa Bell, an' he sure waren't no faster. Satch told about one time Cool Papa flipped out the light switch at the door of their hotel room an' got in the bed 'fore the light went out. He was that fast."

"No kiddin', that really happened. What Cool Papa said about it, though, was there was a short in the light switch that made the light delay in turnin' out. Satch thought it was funny an' made a big deal outta tellin' it all over the league. I tell you what, though, Cool Papa never hardly got throwed out stealin' second.

"They called Josh Gibson the black Babe Ruth. He hit as many home runs as Babe Ruth an' knocked 'em farther an' didn't strike out near as much as Babe did."

Big Ike was speechless, but his eyes were not.

It was on that trip my father lost his patience with the Jim Crow ways of the South. They were in the little town of Tupelo about eighteen miles from Newport at noon. Big Ike stopped at a little country store and café. He invited Bud to come in with him to buy a bologna sandwich and soda pop.

Bud was hesitant, but he did as he was told. They took their seats at a table and waited to be served. The man behind the counter made no move to serve them.

Big Ike spoke up and said, "How 'bout some service here, friend."

The man said nothing for a moment and then said, "I'll wait on you, but I ain't servin' no colored."

Bud started to rise, but Big Ike stopped him. "You'll serve this one," he said.

"The hell I will," was the reply.

Big Ike got up and walked toward the counter. The man reached under the counter. When his hand appeared, it was holding a wicked looking billy club.

Big Ike said, "You don't need the club, mister, 'cause I ain't gonna hit you. But I'll say this. If you lift that club up off the bar I'm gonna take it away from you and stick it up your ass."

The man left the billy club on the bar, but he kept his hand on it.

"Buck Harper owns this building and you rent it from him, don't you? Also, about ninety percent of your business in this store comes from Buck," said Big Ike.

The man made no reply. Big Ike went to the phone on the wall, cranked the bell handle on it and lifted the earpiece. When the operator asked for the number, Big Ike said, "Ring me up Buck Harper's gin."

In a moment Big Ike said, "Buck, this is Ike Wood here. I'm thinkin' I'm gonna be makin' near 'bout three thousand bales of cotton this year."

There was a pause, and then Ike continued, "That's true, Buck. Say, I'm gettin' a lot of pressure to split up my ginnin' business an' give Joe Taylor 'bout half my cotton this year."

Another pause — this one longer. Then Ike continued, "Aw hell, Buck, you know I ain't gonna take none of my business away from you. One more thing, though. This chicken shit in this little Tupelo store you own says he don't wanta serve my colored man no dinner. What about that?"

After a pause, Ike held the receiver out to the man and said, "He wants to speak to you."

The man took the receiver and put it to his ear. After listening for a minute, he hung up and turned to Bud and Big Ike, saying, "What can I serve you, gentlemen?"

After my grandfather died, Big Ike was left with the responsibility of managing all of his family's farms, leaving him less time for those car trips with Bud. In turn, Bud shouldered almost total responsibility of running the Jacksonport farm. He ran it profitably for Big Ike. Bud was almost forty years old, and his old wrist injury was more bothersome than ever. His fingers became gnarled from untreated fractures sustained in baseball games and years of heavy farm labor.

The Jacksonport farm prospered as did all the other Wood farms. With World War II came a steady demand for cotton. Bud's farm always made at least a bale an acre. Utah worked for him year round, and in times of heavy demand, Hillard, Junior and all their brothers and sisters worked the fields as well.

It was the winter of forty-one that Big Ike moved us — his wife and children — to Newport. We settled in the house at 19 Third Street.

As the war progressed and rationing made sugar, coffee and other foods scarce, Big Ike had Bud raise corn, tomatoes, okra, and beans on forty acres of the Jacksonport farm. His vegetables were prized by many housewives in Newport, Tuckerman and Jonesboro, including my mother, who spent her summers canning, pickling and preserving.

War-driven demand for farm products spurred Big Ike to buy more land to grow more crops. The expansion required money Ike didn't have. He turned to the banks for loans, but their losses during the recent Depression made the local bankers tight with their money.

Big Ike figured the best way to borrow money from a banker was to make him think he really didn't need the money. When he wanted to buy the Farrell farm in Woodruff County, he borrowed the hundred fifty thousand dollars he needed from the First National Bank in Augusta.

Big Ike donned a seersucker suit, white shoes, white shirt with a navy bow tie and topped it off with a new straw Panama plantation hat. Then he went to Leach's Funeral Home and talked Frank Leach into loaning him his black Cadillac limousine.

He stopped by the Star Clothing Company and picked up a few things and then headed for the Jacksonport farm. Bud didn't know what to think when he saw the limousine drive up.

Big Ike got out coatless and hatless, and said, "Go wash up, Bud, an' come on. We're goin' to Augusta."

"In that?" asked Bud, incredulously.

"Hell yeah. Now hurry up an' do as I say."

So Bud went to the well and washed himself as best he could and came back to the car.

"You got any socks on under those brogans you're wearin," Big Ike asked.

"Naw," said Bud.

"Well go in the house an' get some black socks an' come on," ordered Big Ike.

Bud did as he was told and soon they were on their way, with Big Ike driving and Bud in the front seat with him.

Big Ike tossed a carton of Camels to Bud and said, "Here, I brought you some smokes."

"Thanks," said Bud. "I run out of tobacco yesterday an' been smokin' corn silks since then. Man, I been wantin' a Camel."

"Well, light up an' give me one," said Big Ike.

When they reached the outskirts of Augusta, Big Ike pulled off the road and parked in a pecan grove. "Come on," he said, and the men got out of the car and went around to the rear where Big Ike opened the trunk.

He pulled out a package and said, "Put these on."

Bud opened the package and found a new black suit, black patent shoes, white shirt and black tie, black leather gloves and a snap-brim black cap. Bud laughed and did as he was told.

When he was dressed, Big Ike lit two Camels and gave one to Bud. The two smoked in silence, and when they finished Big Ike looked at Bud and said, "Ready?"

"Ready," replied Bud. Big Ike took a big cigar from inside his coat pocket, unwrapped it and lit it. Then he put on his coat and Panama hat and took a seat in the back of the limousine on the right-hand side. Bud got behind the wheel and started the engine.

"To the First National Bank, Mr. Chauffeur," said Big Ike. "I'm fixin' to borrow me a hundred an' fifty thousand dollars."

Bud drove slowly into town. All eyes on Main Street were on them. When they reached the bank, Bud parked the car, got out, walked around to the right rear door, opened the door and out came Big Ike with the cigar in his mouth, bigger than life.

Bud stood by the car, and Big Ike walked to the bank. One of the bank officers rushed to the door and opened it for him.

Everyone who walked by looked Bud over, and several colored people whistled in admiration. In a few minutes Big Ike came out, cigar in his mouth, solemn as a judge. Bud opened the rear door for him, and he got in and took his seat. Then Bud walked around to the driver's door in a very dignified manner, got in and started the car.

"Home, James," said Big Ike, and off they went.

When they reached the city limits, Big Ike let out a whoop and yelled, "Let her rip, Bud. I got it!"

In early spring of 1945, Bud was nearly killed in a farming accident. He was discing a field, in preparation for the planting season, when he got the tractor too close to a bar ditch. The tractor turned over, rolled into the ditch and rolled over Bud, crushing the left side of his chest.

Bud lay there for several hours in intense pain. He went in and out of consciousness. Finally, he was found by Utah Brown. Utah rode a mule three miles to the nearest phone, where he called an ambulance. Next, he called Big Ike who told him he would meet them at the Newport Hospital.

When Bud was brought into the hospital emergency room, his breathing was shallow and he could not speak. Doctor Jacob Johnson came into the room and examined Bud's injuries, from which nurses had peeled blood-soaked clothing. "There's nothing I can do for this man," Doc Johnson said. "I believe in leaving the dead alone."

"Wait a minute now, Doc," interrupted Big Ike. "I want everything done that is humanly possible to save this man!"

"Ike, this man's got a flail chest on the left. All his ribs are broken. His lung is collapsed. He's as good as dead. The sword of Damocles is off his head now for sure."

"Well, he's still breathin', an' his right lung is okay. If you cain't help him, call in somebody who can."

"I'll do what I can," replied the doctor. With that, he clamped the skin over the front of Bud's left chest, tied gauze to the clamps and pulled the other end of each gauze strip through intravenous stands, elevating Bud's chest.

Immediately Bud began to breathe a little better. Then Dr. Hayden, the surgeon, came in and placed a chest tube in the left side of Bud's chest. That inflated the collapsed lung. Within fifteen minutes, Bud's breathing was smooth and his blood pressure rose to normal. Thirty minutes later, he regained consciousness.

Bud was in the hospital for six weeks. Big Ike paid all his bills. Two months after his discharge, Bud had recovered. To Big Ike it was obvious that he would not be able to do any more heavy farm work. The chest injury, in addition to his arthritic hands, made heavy work all but impossible. Bud hung around the farm and lived in his little house. Occasionally he would ride a mule around the land just to see what Utah, Hillard and Junior were accomplishing.

In spite of his chest injury, he continued to smoke. He smoked Camels when he could get them, and when he couldn't he rolled his own using Prince Albert or Bull Durham.

After a year, Big Ike decided to bring Bud to town. Ike went out to the farm one morning in early June to tell Bud his decision.

"Mornin', Bud," said Big Ike when Bud answered his knock. "How you feelin'?"

"I feel tolerable well, Big Ike. How're you?"

"Fine, Bud, fine. You got some coffee in there?"

"Sure do. Come on in."

They sat for a while enjoying their coffee. Finally Big Ike said, "Bud, old friend, we both know you're not gonna be able to do no more farm work. There is just no way, with your weak lung, bad hands an' all."

"I know it, Big Ike. Give me a day or two, an' I'll clear out of here an' let you have your cabin back."

"Now hold your horses. I ain't about to put you out on your ear.

Here's what I'm leadin' up to. I wanta move you into town an' set you up livin' on my place. I got a room out behind the garage you can live in."

"I don't want no charity, Big Ike. I ain't a total cripple. I'll find me a place an' get me some kinda job," Bud protested.

"Hear me out," Big Ike said. "You can live in my room out back an' keep up my yard. You can also tend my garden. There'll be other stuff around the house, an' you can help Naomi inside the house with heavy housework.

"But most important of all, you can help take care of my boy, Isaac. He's ten years old, an' he needs to learn to do yard work an' other stuff around a house. I don't have time to teach him, so I want you to do it. He can be a mean little snot at times, but he's basically a good boy. I'm askin' you to help us raise him. I sure ain't offerin' you charity."

Bud thought about it awhile and then accepted. I was about to get a new friend and companion.

My mother and Baby Lewis, a black woman who helped her with housework at times and sometimes baby-sat me, cleaned up Bud's room in anticipation of his arrival. They put down a rug and hung curtains. Hand-me-down furniture was collected for Bud's room.

A plumber repaired the toilet adjacent to the room. Bud had to go outside from his room and enter the toilet from its own door on the alley side of the building. A small sink was installed in Bud's room for washing. A wood-burning Franklin stove was installed to be used for heat as well as for cooking. There was no bathtub; Bud would bathe in a washtub.

Bud was to take all his meals in our house. He was to eat in the kitchen after we ate in the breakfast room or dining room. He would receive room and board and five dollars a week.

On the Friday night before the Saturday that Bud was to move in, my parents sat me down in the living room. Dad had taken a drink or two earlier and was beginning to show the change in personality that always accompanied his drinking.

"Son, we're gettin' us a yardman tomorrow by the name of Bud Parrott. He's a little old colored man, and has been working on one of my farms. Me an' Bud gonna make a man outta you. We're gonna teach you how to keep up a yard. One of these days we're gonna teach you to farm.

"Bud's gonna be around here more'n me, and you better mind him. Do whatever he tells you to do, 'cause he's gonna be your boss. Now you understand me, son?"

"Yessir," was all I said. I didn't dare say to my father what I wanted to say — that I didn't want some dumb old colored man telling me what to do. I was intimidated by my father when he was sober — and downright afraid of him when he was drunk. I could tell he was on his way to drunk, and I wasn't about to make him mad, so I said no more.

The next morning about noon Dad drove up in his Studebaker with Bud. As they got out of the car, my dad called me over.

"Isaac," he said, "this is Bud Parrott. Bud, this is my son, Isaac."

"How do, Isaac," said Bud as he extended his right hand.

I looked at the hand and saw the gnarled fingers and the dirty broken nails and was hesitant to shake hands with him.

"Shake hands with Bud, Isaac," my father sternly ordered. I shook his hand and said "hello" and was embarrassed for having hesitated. Bud showed no concern. He just smiled his gentle smile as we shook hands. Then the smile became a grin; and I, at once, became at ease, sure that I had a new and true friend.

After Bud went in his room, my father looked at me coldly and said, "Isaac, don't you never, ever again, hesitate to take a man's hand when he offers it. It doesn't matter if he's white or colored; don't you ever insult a man by refusing to shake his hand. I mean it."

"Yes sir," I said, looking at my shoes.

I had finished the fourth grade that spring. Ever since the first grade, my best friends were Ronnie, Hal and Ricky. Ronnie was handsome, blond and of average size. He was serious, always asking his mother if a behavior was good or bad. He wanted to be sure he behaved — and did — whatever was honorable in her sight.

Hal was red-headed, freckled-faced and a fun-loving cut-up. He could wisecrack to our delight. Hal was a one-kid stand-up act.

Ricky was the brain of our bunch. Had he been born forty years later, he would have been called a nerd. Smart as anything on the inside, he just couldn't shake his awkward image.

I was sort of in the middle. I was lanky, prone to accidents and frequently the butt of Hal's jokes. Though I was accused of being bossy, I considered myself erudite and opinionated.

Hal and Ronnie were athletic. Ricky was quiet and shy; I made the best grades in schoolwork.

All our fathers were farmers. In addition, Ronnie's father sold and repaired tractors, hay balers and combines. Hal's father was the railroad freight agent, and Ricky's father was a cotton buyer. Ricky's family lived in the biggest house and drove the best car, but we all had reasons to count our blessings.

Influenced by the four major allies of the war, we referred to ourselves as "The Big Four." We four were all but inseparable that summer of forty-five. We were at play in my yard in the daytime, but I never invited them there at night when my father might be drinking. Whenever we spent a night together, it was at Ronnie's or Hal's.

Being at my house in the daytime, we all got to know Bud that summer. He was genuinely fond of all of us. Bud played baseball with us and regaled us with stories of Satchel Paige, Cool Papa Bell and Josh Gibson.

We helped Bud in the garden, and he taught us to fish. He had us dig up worms, rigged our cane poles and piled us in my father's Model A fishing car. Bud drove us to an isolated spot back in the Cache River bottoms. Sitting on the bank, we caught bream by the buckets full. We must have fished that spot twenty or thirty times that summer. Our mothers had bream to cook for dinner at least once a week.

That was a glorious summer. The other three members of the Big Four were dear friends, but that summer Bud became my best friend.

Bud's new role as live-in yardman and house boy seemed to cause a change in his relationship with Big Ike. No longer were they employer and employee who were also friends. Now Bud had become a servant, and Big Ike was his master.

There were no longer car trips, shared cigarettes and conversation. Now their relationship consisted of Big Ike giving orders and Bud carrying them out. It seemed the closer Bud and I became, the farther apart he and my father were.

Toward the end of that summer we four boys began going to a bar ditch, across the levee on the other side of the colored section of town, to skinny-dip. We dared not tell our fathers, because we knew that if they found out there would be hell to pay.

Once when we walked past the colored school we were invited to oppose three colored boys of about our age in a game of basketball.

"You white boys wanta stand us three in a game?" the largest boy asked.

"Well, I just betcha we do," replied Hal, "What's you boys' names?"

"I'm Reggie," said the largest boy, "He's Cooper an' he's Moon."

"Well, I'm Hal, an' the others are Ricky an' Ronnie an' Isaac."

The game was to go to twenty, and in no time we were beaten twenty to six. Another game ended with a similar score. By the third game, Ricky and Moon were going at each other pretty hard. The other five of us were amused by it. We started agitating them.

Finally, Moon and Ricky started to fight. Both were awkward, and neither got the upper hand. Cooper started it, and then we all joined in. "Fight, fight, colored an' a white. Fight, fight, colored an' a white," we all chanted. Soon we were all tickled, even Ricky and Moon.

"Aw, hell, let's all go swimmin'," said Hal and we all took off running across the levee to the bar ditch. We took off our clothes and jumped in.

We were having a wonderful time when my father drove up onto the top of the levee, got out of his car and motioned for me to come.

"Get your clothes on and get in the car," he ordered. "An' tell your three buddies to get their asses home."

I did as I was told, and the other three white boys got dressed and began walking toward home atop the levee. Reggie, Moon and Cooper stayed in the water.

On the way home in the car my father said, "Isaac, don't you ever let me catch you messin' around with any of those colored boys again. You hear me now?"

"Why not? They're okay, an' we were havin' fun."

"Son, don't you sass me. I'll tear your ass up. You better mind me, if you know what's good for you."

That was the first time I saw prejudice in my father. I didn't understand, but I knew I was scared.

We, the Big Four, never went back into the colored section of town again. We saw Reggie, Cooper and Moon on the streets, but we never spoke of that day again. They had their world, and we had ours. They went to their school; we went to ours. All of us went to the Friday night movie at the Strand theater. We sat in the main auditorium and they sat in the balcony, where all blacks sat.

Soon we four white friends all but forgot our black friends. Segregation was just the way life was. We never gave it a second thought.

Our spirit of adventure, however, had not left us. Soon it found a new venue: Fortune's Pool Hall on the north end of Front Street. We discovered that a pool hall was a wonderful place. At the front, near the street, was a bar where beer and sandwiches were served. Opposite the bar was a very large blackboard reaching from the floor to the ceiling. On it were posted all the day's national and local sports contests, with betting odds and up-to-date scores added. We hadn't known there was so much interest in betting.

In the back of the building were two rows of game tables. The four nearer the front were snooker tables and the eight at the rear were pool tables.

By my eleventh birthday, we four were entering the pool hall through the alley door and playing eight ball, nine ball, rotation or straight pool. Ronnie and Hal were about equal in skill and far better than Ricky and I.

After weeks of almost daily pool-shooting, we got brave and started using the front door. A week later, a friend of my father spotted us leaving the pool hall and told on us.

Each of us was called on the carpet by his parents. My dad told me if he ever caught me in a pool hall again he would whip my ass until my nose bled. Ronnie's dad lacked graphic vocabulary, but said pretty much the same thing. Hal's dad just laughed about it. Ricky's father used psychology.

He bought Ricky a regulation pool table and had it installed in the empty servants' quarters in their back yard. He then invited all of us to play pool there any time we wanted, figuring this would keep us out of the pool halls.

The psychology worked on Ronnie, Hal and me, for soon we were sick of pool and looking for other entertainments. Ricky, however, became an expert pool shooter. All his free practice time soon paid off. Ricky sneaked back to the pool hall and began playing grown men for money.

His father never found out, and Ricky won much more often than he lost.

The summer of my twelfth year Bud and I were inseparable. At my father's insistence that I help keep up the yard and the garden, I was to work mornings. Afternoons, I was free to run with my friends.

When my parents were away from home, my mother arranged for Baby Lewis to be there to look after me. This rankled Bud considerably, but he was careful not to show it. One morning his patience wore thin, and he finally lost his temper.

My parents were gone on an overnight trip, and Baby Lewis was staying at the house. That morning she was shelling peas while sitting on the back door steps.

I approached her and said, "Baby Lewis, me and Ronnie and Hal are goin' to the picture show tonight. I'll be home about nine-thirty or ten."

"Well now, you be careful downtown, Little Ike." She always called me Little Ike but never in the presence of my parents. "They's some rough folks down there on Saturday night. They liable to cut you, you not careful."

"What you mean, cut me, Baby Lewis? Nobody's ever messed with us at the show."

"They's mean folks, I tell you. Why, no more than a month ago a colored woman buried a ax in the chest of her man. She done it right out in front of the Strand, too. I ain't never goin' downtown without I got my blade with me, 'specially on a Friday or a Saturday night."

"Aw, that was just an old drunk woman mad at her boyfriend. She wouldn't have messed with anybody else," I argued. "And, anyway, what do you mean about havin' your blade with you?"

"Look," she said, and she opened her mouth to show me that her tongue was folded back on itself. She unfolded her tongue and straightened it out to reveal a single-edged razor blade she had hidden in the fold. I was amazed, particularly when I realized she had been able to conceal that blade and talk as plainly as anyone.

"You needs to learn to carry a blade, honey. Here, let me show you how."

Bud came up and saw what was happening. He became angry and yelled, "Baby Lewis, don't you be teachin' that child none of your shit. Now you get your ass outta here an' get on home."

Baby Lewis left, and after Bud told my parents what had happened, she was never allowed back on the place again. In fact, I never saw her again anywhere.

From then on, I never had to have a baby sitter. Whenever my parents left town, Bud moved into the house and stayed until their return. If they went out for an evening, Bud stayed in the house until they arrived, no matter how late it was. Bud became very protective of me, and I looked on him as a friend as well as a mentor.

As we grew older, Ronnie and Hal remained my good friends, although we were no longer constant companions. Ricky drifted away from us. His interests had become more cerebral and ours more athletic.

Hal and Ronnie were star athletes. I longed to be, but I was as awkward as a praying mantis.

Bud took it on himself to teach me to pitch, and he hoped he could make a baseball player of me.

"Grip the ball with your first two fingers across the laces an' your thumb underneath," he would say. Then reach way back an' pull your elbow frontwards 'til it gets even with your shoulder. Then snap your forearm across an' down. That's the way to throw a fastball."

He showed me how to throw a curve, a knuckleball and a screwball; but I was never able to master any of the pitches. I just could not throw a baseball straight.

Finally, we quit trying and just played catch. Sometimes Bud would pitch to me in an attempt to teach me to bat. He was a little more successful at that, and I became a pretty good batter. All the time we were playing, he would tell me tales of Satchel Paige and his baseball days.

One day I told Bud I needed to stop for a while and go inside and take an aspirin.

"What's the matter with you, boy?" he asked.

"I've just got a headache is all," I replied.

I went inside but could find no aspirin. I did find a medicine bottle with my mother's name on it along with the instruction to take one or two as needed for pain. I took two.

Within twenty or thirty minutes my headache was gone. Truthfully, I felt a little giddy. When I went back outside, Bud was hoeing the grass away from the edge of the sidewalk. When he saw I was unsteady on my feet, he asked what was the matter.

"I took two of Mama's pain pills, an' I'm a little dizzy an' a little sick at my stomach," I replied. "My headache's gone, though."

Bud put down his hoe and came over to me and felt my head. Then he sat down in the yard swing and laid me down beside him, my head in his lap. As we slowly swung back and forth, he gently rubbed my head.

"Ikie, you must never, ever take somebody else's medicine. You never know what it's for if'n it's somebody else's. Did I ever tell you what happened to Sixty Nine when he done that?"

"Naw, Bud, what happened to Sixty Nine?" I asked, smart-alecky.

"Well, old Sixty, he was Mr. Hugh Monte's right-hand man. Mr. Hugh Monte raised him from a baby. One time Mr. Hugh Monte had an old boar hog who lost his git up and go. Mr. Hugh Monte told Sixty to go inside the barn an' bring him a bottle that was up on the shelf.

"Sixty done as he was told, an' Mr. Hugh Monte poured about half the medicine in that bottle down the mouth of that hog, an' in no time that old boar hog was as good as new.

"Sixty spoke up an' asked, 'Mr. Hugh Monte,' he says, 'what is that stuff you give that hog?'

"'That's some stuff the vet give me,' he says, 'to make a boar hog act like a boar hog's supposed to act.'

"Now Sixty had a girlfriend, name of Sweet Baby. She could tell he was beginnin' to slip a lot. She begun complainin' and tryin' to get him to go to the doctor, but Sixty would have none of that. So one night Sixty slipped into the barn an' taken him a big swig of the hog medicine.

"Well, it worked just the opposite on Sixty. He slipped even more, and pretty soon he couldn't do no good for Sweet Baby or Mr. Hugh Monte or nobody else. "Finally Mr. Hugh Monte taken him to the doctor, but the doctor couldn't find out what was wrong with him. Sixty never did tell Mr. Hugh Monte what he done.

"Sixty wasn't ever the same man he used to be no more.

"So you see, you better never take no medicine meant for somebody else. Ain't no tellin' what can happen to you if you do."

Most Saturday nights my parents went out, and Bud stayed in the house with me. Whenever he had a free Saturday night he would stay in his room, and after a time he began to drink a little wine. He only drank on Saturday nights, and I could tell on Sunday morning if he had been drinking the night before. Bud always looked hung over after a night of drinking.

Josephine, the maid of one of our neighbors, took a liking to Bud and began to come around on Saturday nights. Usually she would bring a bottle of wine, and Bud would let her in, and they would get drunk together.

At first those nights were peaceful, but after awhile Josephine made demands that Bud had no inclination to meet. Bud never forgot Queenie and never had any desire to turn to another woman.

To Bud, Josephine was just a friend and someone to drink with, nothing more. As time went on, she began to expect and demand more of Bud than he was able to give. That led to drunken fights loud enough to disturb the neighbors.

Finally, they complained to my father. On one occasion, someone actually called the police, who jailed both Bud and Josephine overnight for disturbing the peace.

My father paid their bail that Sunday morning, admonishing them both. "Josephine," he said," I don't want you comin' on my place no more. Now I mean it. You come on my place again an' I'll get Mr. Lofton to fire you for sure."

After she left he said to Bud, "An' you ... look at you. You're a sorry sight. Bud, I'll have no more of this. You keep that woman away from my place. I mean it. You rile the neighbors up any more, an' I won't have any choice but to run you off. You better know I mean it."

"I know, Mr. Wood. I'm sorry for the trouble I caused. You won't have no more trouble from me, an' I won't let Josephine come around no more."

Talk about the pot calling the kettle black! My father could create more of a disturbance with his drinking in a week than Bud could create in a lifetime. To me it just wasn't fair.

For the next couple of years nothing much changed in our lives. Of course, I went through puberty during that time and grew to be a little taller than my father; although I weighed a hundred pounds less.

If Josephine came around anymore none of us saw her, and Bud made no mention of her. As far as I could tell, Bud's drinking came to a complete halt.

My father, however, was another story. His drinking became almost a nightly occurrence. Not only did he drink more often, but he consumed more once he started. He became more violent. I often heard him scream at my mother. Frequently, on the morning after his excess, I found Mother with dark bruises on her neck and arms.

By day he had total amnesia of the night before, and he never had a hangover. When sober he functioned normally. Friends and business contacts had no reason to think him anything other than jovial, competent and affable.

Neither my mother nor I ever confronted him about his drinking when he was sober. We just hoped he would remain sober that night as well. All too often, it was not to be. Not only was I silent to my father about his drinking, but I was silent about it to everyone else, too. Even to Bud.

One night in the summer of forty-nine, I could stand it no more. He had been screaming at my mother for what seemed like hours. I feared he would hurt her. Rather than slip out the window or go the attic, I stayed in my room and listened.

Soon I heard blows, and I went into the hall. My parents were fighting. Mother was trying to defend herself. Father was using her long hair as a handle, whipping her head against the wall. In the wall, I saw a catcher's mitt open as if to catch a long throw. Then I realized it was no mitt, but the indentation left by my mother's head, from his banging her into the wall.

"Stop it, Daddy," I yelled as I ran toward them. "Stop it, I said!"

I grabbed him. I tried to pull him away from her. His fist hit my jaw. The next thing I knew, I was on the floor. Dad released Mother and started toward me, with the fire of rage in his eyes.

"Run, Isaac," Mother yelled.

I started to get up and he swung at me again. He missed. The momentum of his swing caused him to fall, and I had time get to my feet.

"Run, I'll be all right. Hurry," Mother said, more calmly this time.

I ran. He chased me, all the time yelling that he would kill me when he caught me. All I could think of was that I had to get out of that house. The next thing I knew, I was in the back yard, running toward Bud's room.

Bud stood outside his door and motioned for me to come there. Why did he seem calm? Didn't he know the danger? "Get in my room" he said, "Get up in under the bed an' keep quiet."

I did as I was told, and Bud walked out into the darkness to confront my father, who was lumbering across the yard. "What's goin' on, Big Ike?" Bud asked.

"Where's that goddamned boy of mine?" Dad demanded. "Where'd he go? I know you saw him."

"Naw sir, I ain't seen him." Bud lied. "I got just a glimpse of somebody a-runnin' off down yonder toward the bridge, though. It looked like a man in his undershorts."

"That was him. Goddammit. I'll beat the shit outta that little bastard. He tried to hit me."

"Come on now, Big Ike. You ain't in no shape to go chasin' off down the street. Besides, folks'll see you an' call the police. That'd be terrible embarrassin'. I tell you what, let me help you back inside the house. I'll go find the boy an' bring him home."

Beginning to feel weak and nauseous, Big Ike let Bud help him back toward the house. Bud had to stop to let him vomit, but soon they entered the house.

Sooner than I expected, Bud was back in his room. He closed the door quietly and called to me. "It's okay, Ikie. Come on out. Just be quiet."

I crawled out from under the bed and said, "I hope the son of a bitch dies in his sleep. I can't stand much more of this, an' Mama can't either. One of these nights he's gonna kill her."

"Don't talk like that, boy. You don't want your daddy to die. You gotta stop worryin' about your mama. She can take care of herself. Besides, she could leave him if she wanted to.

"They's both good people. They's just sick, that's all," he said.

"My mama isn't sick. It's just him. The son of a bitch!"

"Don't talk like that. I mean it," he said. "Naw, Ikie, you're wrong. They's both sick, an' I ain't so sure but what she ain't sicker than him."

I didn't agree and couldn't understand what he was getting at. I just shut up and went to sleep. Before dawn, Bud woke me and said I needed to go back into the house and get in my own bed.

Both my parents were sleeping in their bed; my father's snoring was audible as soon as I opened the door. In my bed, I laid awake until dawn. As always, my parents awoke to the new day bright and cheerful, as though they had attended a church social the night before.

Things seemed to get better after that night. I had begun to drive, and Dad turned the Model A over to me. It needed painting, so Bud and I decided to paint it dark green.

One afternoon while we were there alone, we used masking tape to protect all the parts that were not to be painted. Bud rigged a spray painting apparatus by hooking the hose of my mother's vacuum cleaner to the exhaust end of the canister. He took the top off a spray can and adapted it to the threaded part of a Mason jar. Then he filled the Mason jar with green paint.

When we plugged in the vacuum cleaner, we had an efficient spray painting system. In no time, the Model A looked as good as new.

Having transportation, I was able to stay out later at night and cover more ground. Ronnie and Hal rode along almost every night. We explored country roads, rode around aimlessly, or just sat in front of the Farm Drive Inn, the local teen hangout. We always saw friends there.

The only time we weren't together every night was when Brenda Langston came from St. Louis for her annual month-long visit with her grandmother. Those nights, only Brenda rode in the Green Monster with me.

In early August of forty-nine, the Model A had a flat tire; and Dad let me take out his forty-seven Roadmaster Buick, his pride and joy. Hal, Ronnie and I were riding around when another car passed us and splattered us with eggs. In retaliation, we went to Hal's house and took all the eggs from his refrigerator. Soon we were in a full-fledged egg war, which finally ended about midnight.

Hal was spending the night with Ronnie, and when I dropped them off I noticed dry egg yolk all over the outside of the car. I knew I was in deep trouble if something wasn't done; so I drove down our alley with the lights off, stopped and got out and knocked on Bud's door.

"What's the matter with you, boy? Don't you know what time it is?" Bud asked as he wiped the sleep out of his eyes. "I'm in deep trouble, Bud. Look at Daddy's car."

"Good God a'mighty. Y'all been egg-fightin'. Damn, boy, don't you know egg'll take the paint off of a car?"

"Oh, shit," I said.

"Come on," said Bud as he got in the car. Let's us go down to the Esso station at the corner of Beech an' Third. Clell Eaves stays in the back of the station. I'll wake him up, an' we'll wash the car."

We worked on that car until three-thirty, and it was spotless. I sneaked into the house an hour before my parents awoke, and they never found out what happened.

Dad noticed later in the week some areas where small flecks of paint had come off the car. He complained to the Buick dealer that the paint job was defective. The dealer repainted the whole car free of charge.

The Friday before football practice was to start on Monday, my parents left town for a long weekend and left Bud in charge. About noon, I suggested to Bud that we go fishing on the Cache River.

Ronnie and Hal were nowhere to be found, so Bud and I piled in the Green Monster and headed for the river. We drove about a mile down a river bottom road through the woods to a place Bud had fished a few years earlier.

When we got out of the car and made our way through the underbrush to the river, I felt as though we were crawling through a jungle. The underbrush was thick, the day was hot and the mosquitoes were vicious. I was tempted to suggest we leave; but then the brush cleared, revealing the river and its shaded bank. It was dark, peaceful and much cooler than in town.

We rigged our poles and sat on the bank, watching our corks bobbing in the water. After an hour of no luck, Bud decided to move.

"There ain't enough room for two of us in this hole, Ikie," he said. "You go on fishin' here, an' I'm gonna move a couple of hunnerd yards downstream to another hole I know. If I have any luck I'll holler for you."

After about an hour, I started catching fish. I caught eight or nine big bream and then a couple of slab crappie. I began to laugh out loud at the thought of Bud going off by himself and coming up empty.

I was just pulling out my third big crappie, when I felt a terrible pain in the back of my head. Everything went black. At some point, I was aware of being moved, but I felt and saw nothing. It was as though I was floating in a dark room.

When my mind began to clear, I realized I was sitting with my back leaning against a tree. I tried to move, but couldn't. My vision was blurry, but I was aware of someone or something a few feet in front of me. Soon I realized I was tied to the tree.

Struggling did not help. As my vision cleared, I could see a gaunt white man squatting on his haunches six or eight feet in front of me.

"Won't do you no good to holler, boy. Ain't nobody 'round to hear you. Go ahead an' holler, though. I like to hear hollerin'," he said.

I was very scared, but I knew I had to keep my wits about me. "Why are you doing this to me?" I asked, "I haven't done anything to you."

"Oh, yes you have. You've invaded my home. You've caught my fish. You cain't do things like that to me."

He got up and walked about aimlessly. He was tall, thin and dressed in dirty tattered clothes. His eyes were deep set and dark; and the hollows of his eyes were almost black, giving him a piercing, crazy look. His long black hair was flecked with gray. A scraggly beard, more gray than black, nearly reached his belly. His lips, partially hidden by the beard, seemed more blue than pink. His teeth were broken, dirty and carious. What facial skin that I could see was dirty and splotched by large blackheads. Tobacco stains ran from his teeth to his beard and onto his clothes.

His skeletal hands bore a sheen of translucent skin tautly stretched over bone. His nails, ragged and crusted with dirt, looked unhuman. In his left hand was a whetstone; in his right, the longest knife I had ever seen.

Squatting beside me, all the while rubbing the knife on the stone, he paused occasionally only to spit on the stone.

"Scream, boy. I wanta hear you scream. You took from me, an' now you gotta pay. Scream, I said!" He slapped me across the face with the broad side of the knife blade and yelled, "Scream, you son of Delilah. I wanta hear you beg and scream!"

God knows I wanted to scream, but if I did, Bud would come running and be killed. I knew I was doomed. Prayer was the only recourse, so silently, tears streaming down my face, I prayed.

"I said scream," he slapped me again with the knife. "Scream, god ..."

I heard the blow but did not see it. When I looked up, the man lay unconscious at my feet. Bud stood over him, a bloody club in his hand.

The look in Bud's eyes was so intense and angry, it scared me almost as much as the crazy man had. With one motion, Bud bent down, picked up the knife and slit my tormentor's throat from ear to ear. Blood. More blood than I have ever seen spewed from the gash. That evil man was dead.

"Good God, Bud," I cried as he untied me. "You killed that man!"

"That I did," he said calmly, "There's no way I was gonna let that animal live. We woulda had to of looked over our shoulders the rest of our lives. I waren't about to let that happen."

I knew he was right. "We gotta go get the sheriff," I said.

"No we don't!" Bud exclaimed. "This here dead fiend is a white man. I'm a no 'count colored. No matter what I say or you say, they'll make me pay for killin' a white man."

"What'll we do then?" I asked.

"You ain't gonna do nothin'. I am," he said. "You got any money?"

"A couple of dollars."

"You go get in the Model A an' go into the store at Amagon. Buy a gallon of coal oil. Anybody ask you what you need that much for, tell 'em the football boys is gonna have a big bonfire. Then come straight back to where we parked the car, an' I'll be waitin' for you."

I did as I was told, and when I returned Bud was there waiting as he had promised.

"Did they ask you anything?" Bud asked.

"No."

"Good. Now go home an' get me the spade and the ax that's in your daddy's garage. Go in my room and bring them coveralls that looks like a train engineer's clothes. Don't stop to talk to nobody an' don't waste no time."

I returned in half an hour. Bud wasn't there. I was about to panic when he suddenly emerged from the woods.

"Okay, Ikie, you listen to me, son. You go on home an' act like nothin' has happened. Don't tell nobody nothin'. Now, I mean that. If anybody asks where I'm at, you tell 'em I'm probably off drunk somewheres.

"It's near 'bout suppertime now. You go into Fred's or the Bridge Cafe an' get you a couple of hamburgers. Then go have a good time with them buddies of yours. Act normal. Don't tell nobody nothin'.

"I may not show up 'til Sunday, but I'll be there 'fore your folks gets home. An' one more thing, when you leave here, from now to forever more, we ain't never, ever gonna talk about it no more. We ain't never gonna mention this again. Now you understand me?"

"Yessir," I replied.

"Don't 'sir' me, son. Now get gone!"

I got in the Model A and left. In the rearview mirror, I watched Bud watching me. I knew that Bud and I would never be the same again.

The next forty-eight hours were miserable. I feared that if I looked up Ronnie or Hal, they would sense something was wrong. Not telling them would be the hardest. Ronnie might keep my secret, but I wasn't sure about Hal. The only way was to tell neither one. It would remain between Bud and me.

My parents absence was a relief. They were not there to notice Bud's absence. By the time they were to return, I hoped my nerves would be settled.

I stayed in the house. I didn't answer the telephone. Twice, I walked to the Bridge Cafe for a hamburger. Otherwise, it was cereal out of the box and silence. The house was never so small.

All day Saturday and Saturday night I was alone. The longer he was away, the more I feared something had happened to Bud. I dared not go back to the river bottoms.

Bud should not have killed that man. He should have tied him up and gone for the sheriff. But he did the only thing he could imagine to do — he saved my life. I knew Bud was right when he said that if we had turned the man over to the law, we would have to always watch our backs. If the law took him, he would probably get ninety days in the State Mental Hospital and then be turned loose.

Bud was also right when he called that man an animal. And had we gone to the sheriff after killing him, Bud would not have survived the "justice" he would have received. Knowing all this, I decided my only viable course of action was to keep my mouth shut.

My sentence: no sleep Friday night; only fitful sleep Saturday night. Bud was not home by noon Sunday, and I began to panic. A couple of minutes before two o'clock I saw him walking up the alley.

"Bud!" I called out as I ran toward him. "Is everything okay?"

He just held up his hand for me to be quiet. Calmly he said, "Everything's all right, an' it's gonna stay all right. You remember what I told you. There'll be no more said about it. Never!"

Bud went to his room and I to mine. Two hours later my parents returned. For the next few days, I didn't see Bud, except in passing.

Football practice started, and then school. The routine was a relief. Bud was quieter than ever. He came out of his room less and less. I noticed empty wine bottles in the alley outside his room. At times I smelled wine on his breath. Coming in late one Saturday night, I saw a woman resembling Josephine leaving his room.

Like the continents we studied, Bud and I were drifting apart. Our secret wasn't the sort of thing that would cement our friendship. While Bud's life was slowing down, mine was speeding up. Girls. Football. Term papers. His continent was not moving in my direction, and mine was picking up speed.

The following summer I saw Brenda again when she came from St. Louis to visit her grandmother. We were together almost every day for a month. Then she went home.

The first week of August, I talked Ronnie into going to St. Louis to see the Cardinals play the Pittsburgh Pirates. Dad loaned us his car and we stayed in a hotel close to Sportsman's Park. I phoned Brenda the day we arrived. She was going steady with a classmate, but she did invite me to her home for dinner.

Ronnie went to the ballgame and saw Stan Musial get four hits, including a home run, while I got to share a meal with Brenda, her parents and her new boyfriend. That dinner was the last time I saw Brenda. To make matters worse, Ronnie spent half the night telling me all about the Cardinals and Stan the Man.

The next night we saw the Cardinals and the Pirates play again. It was Pirates nine to nothing, and Stan Musial went hitless.

The next afternoon the Browns were playing. I had heard about their star, Satchel Paige, from Bud, so I wanted to see him play. Ronnie was all for it.

Our seats were close to the Browns' bullpen. Our eyes were on Satch. Ever consistent, the Browns wilted early. During the third inning, Satch brought a reclining lawn chair out into the sunlight and stretched out for a nap.

I went to the railing and called his name several times, receiving only a casual wave for my efforts.

In desperation I yelled, "Hey, Mr. Paige, Bud Parrott said to tell you 'hello.'"

With that he got up and came over to the rail. "You know Bud Parrott, boy?" he asked.

"Yes sir, I sure do. He works for my daddy and lives on our place," I replied.

"How's he doin'?" asked Satchel.

"Just fine."

"What's your name, son?" he inquired.

"Isaac Wood."

"Well Isaac, you be good to Bud. He's one of the best fellers I ever knew. A hell of a ball player, too. Maybe the best second baseman I've ever seen. If he'd been born ten years later, he would have played in the majors for sure. He was that good.

"Losin' his family the way he did, though, he probably wouldn't of played no white ball nohow."

"What do you mean? I don't know anything about any family."

"That'd be like Bud not to tell nobody. Maybe I shouldn't neither. You know him pretty good, boy?"

"Yes sir. We've been real close friends, and he's done a lot for me. He tried to make a pitcher out of me, but I wasn't any good."

"I'm gonna tell you this 'cause you're his friend, but I'd just as soon you not tell him I did.

"Back in thirty-five me an' Bud was playin' for the Pittsburgh Crawfords. We won the pennant an' played the New York Cubans in the Negro World Series. 'Fore the series, some gamblers tried to get Bud to throw a game to make sure the Cubans won.

"Well, Bud wouldn't do it. In fact, he knocked in the winnin' run to win the deciding game. Them gamblers broke his arm an' burned down his house. His wife an' his little twin boys burned up in the fire. That's when Bud left Pittsburgh and baseball for good."

I couldn't say anything and felt myself about to cry. Even Ronnie was moved almost to tears.

"Yeah, it was sad. I been wonderin' about Bud. You say he's doin' okay?" Satchel asked again.

"He's fine," was all I could say.

Satchel Paige gave each of us an autographed baseball. Satch asked that we give his regards to Bud, but Ronnie said we'd best never mentioned our visit with Satchel to Bud. I agreed. If Bud wanted us to know about his family, he would have told us.

We got back to Newport late that Sunday night. Parting company at Ronnie's house, we resolved to tell no one what we had learned about Bud.

I drove home down Second Street; and when I turned into the alley leading to the back of our house, I noticed there were no lights on in Bud's room. When I got to his room, I saw that the door was ajar so I called out to him.

There was no answer. I entered the room and saw it was empty of all Bud's possessions. All that remained in the room was the used furniture that my mother and Baby Lewis had put there years before.

I ran to the house, and found my father passed out drunk on the couch in the living room. My mother was reading in bed.

"Mama, where's Bud?"

"Come sit down on the bed, Isaac. How was your trip?" she asked.

"Fine, but where's Bud?"

"He and Josephine got into a drunken brawl last night, and your daddy had to ask him to leave. He moved out this morning," she replied.

"No! Where did he go?"

"I don't know, honey. He just took his things and left."

At that moment, I truly hated my father. His drunkenness had made my life miserable for years. Now he had driven away the one person who made life in that house tolerable. What made it even worse was that I knew my father could never be made to understand or regret the pain he'd caused.

Early the next morning, I went looking for Bud. I ran into James, the hot tamale man, who told me Bud had moved to Madame Lena's boarding house. I went there and knocked on the door.

"What you want, child?" asked Madame Lena when she opened the door.

"I need to see Bud Parrott," I replied.

"Upstairs, first door on the right," she said.

When I knocked on Bud's door he called out, "Come on in, Ikie. I figured you'd be comin'."

"I'm gonna talk to Daddy," I said. "I'm gonna talk to him today while he's sober and get him to let you come home."

"No you ain't, boy. Now you listen to me. It's time I left there. Your daddy's done already been by here this mornin'. He give me some money, an' he fixed it up where I can be the janitor at the high school. I'll be okay.

"Don't you be mad at your daddy now. He's a good man. He's got the whiskey sickness, but under it all he's a good man. He loves you, an' he's proud of you, too. Besides, he's doin' right by me."

"But I don't want to lose you, Bud. You take care of me. You're my friend."

"Isaac, you don't need nobody to take care of you. You are near 'bout a man now. You can take care of yourself. An' I'll always be your friend.

"Boy, you done growed up. Your friends need you now. Have fun an' be happy. I'll see you over at the schoolhouse. I'll get to watch you play football an' basketball for free, 'cause I'll be working there.

"This'll be better for me, an' for you. Get along, now. I'll be seein' you around."

So I did as he said and left. I would have two more years at home, and during that two years I was to see Bud only in passing. He was right; I was nearly grown.

For the next two years, I saw Bud almost daily at the high school. We never had much to say to each other. Occasionally, each of us would inquire how the other was doing. Sometimes at football or basketball practice, I would notice Bud standing by himself watching me, but I never saw him at a game.

At school, Bud always wore khakis and a brown paper military-style cap. Over those two years, he began to look frail and much older. Whenever we spoke, I noticed his voice had become husky, and later, hoarse. When I asked about his hoarseness, he said it was from too much Prince Albert.

Most days, though, I didn't think of Bud. I just did my own thing, marking time until I could leave home for college. Farming had lost its appeal for me, and so had life in Newport.

Graduation day finally arrived in June of 1953. Preparation for college consumed that summer. Bud was out of sight, out of mind until the day before I was to leave for college.

All my things were packed and ready to be loaded in the blue Nash Rambler my parents had given me for graduation. Starting my life away from my father's alcoholism was first in my mind. However, on that day, I was already beginning to miss Mother, our house and the comfort of Newport.

After washing my car, I jumped in and drove around town for one last look at all the memorable places of my childhood. As I drove through Remmel Park toward the high school, I saw Bud mowing the football practice field.

Wanting to tell Bud goodbye, I stopped, bounded out of the car and walked across the grass toward him. When Bud saw me, he stopped the mower, grinning from ear to ear. He waved and began to walk toward me.

"Hi, Ikie," he said as we met. "I knowed you'd come to tell old Bud goodbye 'fore you went off to college."

Bud's voice was throatier than ever, and he was even more frail than ever; but his smile and his grin were unchanged. Bud pointed to a tree on the edge of the field. We walked there and sat on the ground in the shade. Bud leaned against the tree and wiped his face with a blue bandana. His paper cap was soaked with sweat, and when he removed it, I was surprised to see how bald he had become.

"What happened to your hair, Bud?" I laughed.

"My brains ate it up," he replied. "Boy, you sure have growed up. You put a little meat on them bones, an' you'll be some kinda man.

"Well, you're finally gettin' outta here, ain't you? I reckon you're happy to be goin'."

"Yeah, I am; but I'm also a little sad, too. I don't know why."

"I knows how you feel. When I left here back in 1919, I felt the same way. It didn't last long, though. This time tomorrow you'll feel fine."

"I hope so," I replied. We were silent for a moment, and then I asked the question that had been burning my brain for the last two years.

"Bud," I said, "I know we said we'd never say anything about what happened down in the river bottoms two years ago, but I just have to ask. What did you do after I left?"

He was quiet for a moment and then he spoke. "I guess you got a right to know, so I'll tell you. But I don't want to ever hear no more about it. Okay?"

"I promise I won't ever say any more to you or to anybody else," I replied.

"That was one crazy man. While you was gone for the ax an' the spade, I looked around, an' I found where he was stayin'. He was livin' in a holler log. He had an old dirty blanket in it an' a tarp over it. Inside he had some papers an' stuff an' a fruit jar full of fingers he had done pickled.

151

"I went back an' got him an' drug him back to his log. Then I went back an' cleaned up all signs of him, an' us, back on the river bank. I figured you'd be back with the tools by then, and sure 'nuff you were.

"After I got the tools I went back to where he was at, an' I taken the ax an' chopped that holler log into a million pieces. Then I taken his clothes off of him, an' I taken his knife an' your daddy's ax an' I taken him apart at all his joints."

"Good God Almighty," I exclaimed.

"I know, but I had to get rid of him. By then it was near 'bout mornin'. I rested awhile, an' then I dug a hole about seven foot deep. It was so deep I had a hard time climbin' out of it.

"I cleared off a place next to the hole an' piled what was the rest of his log an' a bunch of dead wood an' leaves up where I had cleared off. Then I put him, or else the pieces of him, on the pile an' doused the whole thing with coal oil. After that I piled a bunch more logs an' stuff on top an' set the whole thing afire.

"It burned the whole day, an' I slept some while it was burnin'. By night nothin' was left but his skull an' bones. I shoveled everything into the hole an' scraped the ground, where the fire was, clean. Then I covered up the hole an' scattered leaves an' limbs on it. When I was through, nobody could tell anything had ever happened there. Then I walked home."

We sat for the longest in silent reflection. When we finally spoke again our conversation was about happy times and old friends.

Bud asked, "Well, what you plan to study up at that big college? What you gonna make of yourself?"

"I don't know yet," I replied.

"Well you gotta have a goal. One time there was two boys fixin' to cross a pasture filled with snow. One of them boys bet the other'n he could walk a straighter line through the snow. The other'n took him up on it, an' they taken off across the field.

"When they got to where they was goin', the first one's tracks was crooked as they could be, but the second one's was straight as an arrow. When the first one asked the second one how he done it, he said, 'You kept your eyes on the ground a-watchin' your step. I never took my eyes off'n a big tree across the field. I just walked right straight to it.'

"You see, Ikie, the second one had a goal."

We sat awhile longer before I got up to leave. As we walked toward the Rambler, I admitted to Bud that I was afraid I might not make it in college. I might not be smart enough or tough enough.

"Isaac," he said, and I turned toward him, "that reminds me of working in the steel mill in Pittsburgh. We took iron, which is soft for a metal, put it to the fire, an' when it got hot enough for us to cool it down, then it was steel. Steel is the hardest metal there is.

"Boy, what you been livin' through all these years here; that's your fire. You been put to the fire, an' it didn't burn you up. It made you strong like steel. There cain't nothin' break you now."

I waved and turned away so he couldn't see if I began to cry. Those were the last words we ever spoke to each other.

College was a revelation a day. My grades didn't cause any cussing when they arrived in the mail box back home. By the end of my first semester, I decided to work toward a degree in business and become a stockbroker. I had my goal.

Rachel, my future wife, laughed her way into my life one day as I sat waiting for an economics class to begin. To quote the campus radio deejay, the world was my barbeque, and I wasn't sparing the slaw. Then a letter arrived from my mother.

She started off telling me about what was happening at home and how all my friends and relatives were doing. It is the end of her letter that I will remember forever:

> "I hate to have to tell you this, but your old friend, Bud Parrott, has died.
>
> Apparently, he had known he had throat cancer for some time and told no one. Dr. Johnson said it was inoperable anyway, and there was nothing anyone could have done.
>
> They found his body last Monday morning in his bed at Madame Lena's. He died in his sleep, peacefully I am sure. He was buried in the colored cemetery. Your daddy went to his funeral.
>
> I'm sorry.
>
> Love,
> Mother"

Bud was gone, and he died like he had been forced to live — alone. I hadn't been there for him, nor had I even gone to his funeral.

I felt guilty for not having said goodbye. But the more I thought it over, it occurred to me that by not saying goodbye maybe he could stay with me, in spirit, always.

I awoke at midnight, remembering that Rachel and our granddaughter had expected a call from me at bedtime. Sleeping so long reclined against the mulberry stump hadn't been good for my neck or back, but I was alert, refreshed and surprisingly peaceful.

A full moon illuminated the cloudless sky. I wandered around the yard in the moon's white light. The place had changed since my youth, but some of the pecan trees that had been mature fifty years earlier were still there. I remembered cracking pecans with my teeth while sitting beneath those trees.

Peaceful was not what I expected to feel, back in my old hometown. Surprised by the abiding sense that things had turned out as they should, an aching joint or two seemed a small price to pay. I came to realize that, in the past few days, I had buried my ghosts. Hardest of all to reconcile was the ghost of my father. For the first time in many years, I felt released from my anger that had bordered on hatred. Dad had been sick, "the whiskey sickness" as Bud had called it.

One ghost remained to be buried — Bud's ghost. As long as I left his grave unattended, he would not rest. After calling Rachel and returning to the motel, I could not sleep. Memories of those long-ago days with Bud kept intermingling with dreams of the future. My head was a battleground. At four o'clock, I slipped outside and sat in a deck chair beside the pool. As I watched the predawn in the eastern sky and then the sunrise of the new day, I formulated a plan.

When the First National Bank opened at ten o'clock I was there asking to see the president. I was introduced to a dignified man of about seventy who invited me into his office. His name was Thomas Cherry.

"Mr. Cherry," I said, "I'm a stockbroker in St. Louis, and I grew up here in Newport."

"I know, Mr. Wood," he said. "I knew your father. He did business with this bank back when I was just starting out here. I didn't know him well, I'm sorry to say.

"You are modest when you refer to yourself as a stockbroker. If I'm not mistaken you own the I. H. Wood Company in St. Louis."

"True," I admitted, "but that is not why I'm here today. I want to pay my respects to a long-dead black friend buried in an unmarked grave in the Negro cemetery.

"I don't know who is in charge of the cemetery, so I'll need to find that out. Then I want to get permission to bring in a landscape architectural firm from St. Louis to correct all the neglect and make the cemetery presentable.

"I plan to establish an endowment fund to maintain the cemetery in perpetuity. I would like for someone in your bank to act as administrator of the endowment."

"I think your plan is very commendable and will be most appreciated. This bank will be happy to help, and I have just the man to administer your plan."

He picked up his phone and rang an extension. "Mr. Brown," he said into the phone, "could you come to my office, please?"

In a moment a tall, graying athletic-looking black man in his late sixties entered the office.

"Mr. Wood," Cherry said, "this is Reginald Brown, one of our vice presidents. Reginald, Mr. Wood grew up in Newport. He's here about the Negro cemetery."

He explained what I had proposed, and then he spoke to me. "Reginald is a member of the Beulah Land AME Church. His church has charge of the cemetery. I'm sure Mr. Brown will be happy to administer your endowment."

"Of course I will, Mr. Wood," said Brown. "Why don't we meet at the cemetery about one o'clock this afternoon and talk over your ideas. There is something I would like to show you out there."

I went back to the motel, packed my car and checked out. After having a sandwich at the motel restaurant, I drove out to the cemetery. Reginald Brown was waiting for me.

He was carrying an old box wrapped in cellophane and bound with twine. He greeted me and asked me to follow him to the center of the cemetery.

We stopped by a broken holly tree, and he called me by my first name and said, "Isaac, this is Bud's grave. It isn't marked. There was no money. But rest assured, it is his grave. My father was his best friend, and he brought me here often."

"Brown," I said. "Utah Brown! Is Utah your father?"

"He was. He's been dead for fifteen years."

"I'm sorry," I said. "Reginald Brown. My God, you're Reggie, the kid I played basketball and went swimming with."

"That I am," he said.

"Well I'll be," I said. "It's a small world."

"Indeed." he replied. Then he nodded toward the box, "When Bud was in his last few days he gave this box to my dad. He told him he was afraid he would die before he saw you again. He said that when you heard about him you'd come, and when you did he wanted Dad to give you this box.

"Before my dad died he gave me the box. He told me to give it to you if you ever came. I asked him if I couldn't just send it to you; and he said no, that you'd have to come after it. He said if you didn't come, you didn't deserve it.

"Well, you came. It took you long enough, but you came. Here's the box. I suspect it holds all of Bud's possessions."

I took the box but could say nothing. Reggie told me to let him know what I needed done, and then he left.

Back at my car, I sat the box on the hood. For the longest I just stared at it. Finally, I was able to open it.

Inside were two baseballs, one autographed by Ty Cobb and the other by Satchel Paige, Cool Papa Bell, Josh Gibson and several other members of the Pittsburgh Crawfords. There was also an old baseball glove.

In the bottom of the box were several old fragile tablets, the diaries of Sunshine Sam.

Over the next year, the renovation of the cemetery was completed, the progress dutifully overseen by Reggie Brown.

During that time, I turned my brokerage firm over to my daughter whose keen business sense I had always admired. Both my sons were lawyers and partners in a large firm. My daughter had been with me in the brokerage firm since graduating from college.

After retirement, my wife and I began to travel. We planned to retrace the travels of Sunshine Sam, only not live in boxcars. His chronicles would be our guide.

The next summer we went back to Newport to admire the cemetery. As we drove up, I immediately noticed changes. What was once an unkempt lawn was now immaculately tailored.

All the old tombstones had been restored and righted. Each unmarked grave had a small white granite marker ten inches wide and eighteen inches tall. All except one were blank. The one over Bud's grave had a tiny B.P. engraved at its base.

In the middle of the cemetery was a small flower garden surrounded by park benches. In the center of the garden was a brick column four-feet square and four-feet high. On the eastern side of the column was a bronze plaque that said:

"This is the final resting place of
BUD PARROTT
A kind man, a good man, a dear friend."

Atop the column was a life-size bronze statue of two figures. One was a young boy of ten or twelve. He was barefoot and had a baseball glove strapped through his belt. The other was a small man dressed in a shirt, trousers and brogan shoes. He stood next to the boy and to his left. On the man's head was a military-style cap and at his feet lay a baseball bat. In his left hand was a yard broom. His right arm was around the boy's neck, the hand resting gently on the boy's right shoulder.

The two figures looked toward the eastern horizon, as though they were looking at the dawn of a new day.

Inspecting the features of the two faces, one would recognize the boy as white and the man as black. Actually, neither was black nor white; but both were bronze. I wished that life could imitate that art.